Stuck on You

**Book #1 in The Stoneworths Series
by Michelle Stimpson**

Dedication

With love and affection for my grandfathers, my father, my uncles, my brothers, my husband and my son who is now a young man. I'm honored to know such wonderful men.

Acknowledgments

Much gratitude to the Lord for the opportunity to write for Him. I'm forever grateful to have exchanged lives with You according to Matthew 16:25. Life in You is waaaay better!

For my readers to continue to support this wild dream of mine to write books and minister through stories—you encourage me with your emails, posts and tags. I'm honored to know you, even if it's mostly through all these characters!

Special thanks to CaSandra McLaughlin for reading the first draft and finding that cute couple for the cover! To LaSheera Lee, April Barker, and Tia McCollors for your book cover critique. I'm indebted to Paulette Nunlee and Rose Morgan for offering your editorial eyes.

I studied several authors to see how to do this whole "family saga" thing, including Brenda Jackson and Pat Simmons. Thank you for paving the way.

Finally, to my family—thanks for giving me up during part of the holidays so that I could finish writing. Well, you all were asleep most of the time, but hey—you're still good sports!

Be blessed!

Chapter 1

"Gather 'round now, so I can tell the story," one of the oldest living Stoneworths, Uncle Bush, announced from the lazy chair.

Someone in the kitchen switched off the household intercom system, which had been pumping upbeat gospel tunes throughout the two-story mini-mansion. Glasses ceased to clink. Silverware ceased to chink against the fine China that Uncle Bush's wife, Aunt Vera, had proudly used to serve her husband's annual birthday dinner. This birthday was extra special, marking his eighth decade of life.

Braxton Stoneworth gave up his seat on the comfy leather couch nearest Uncle Bush so that the younger ones could get close to hear their story—the Stoneworth legacy—which had been passed down for more than a hundred years now.

His five-year-old first cousin once-removed, Lauren, and her friend quickly scrambled to claim Braxton's empty spot.

Ace, one of the kids from Uncle Shiloh's clan, came running into the family room but stopped short, having been beaten by the girls. "No fair! She's not even a Stoneworth!" He pointed at Lauren's friend.

Lauren's mom, Paige, gently lowered Ace's arm since the boy wasn't practicing good manners at the moment. "You never know, Ace. She might be a

Stoneworth someday."

His brows furrowed in indignation as he crossed his arms on his chest. Little Ace looked like he wanted to say something, but he knew better than to talk back to his aunt, especially in front of the room full of people who would put him in check for saying anything remotely disrespectful to an elder. Simply put: Stoneworths didn't play that.

"Come on, lil' dude. I've got a seat right here for ya." Braxton's oldest brother, Knox, rolled a chair up right next to Uncle Bush.

Ace's expression shined with victory. "Thank you! Thank you! Thank you!"

"You know Stoneworths look out for each other," Knox said, giving Ace some dap.

The brown-skinned boy with bright hazel eyes hopped into the chair, set one tiptoe against the floor, then whirled the seat around for two full 360-degree circles. He raised his hands in the air. "Look at me! I'm flying!"

The room full of Stoneworths and friends filled with soft laughter as brothers, aunts, uncles, and cousins witnessed Ace's antics. Somehow, they had all known that Ace would abuse the rolling chair. He was, as Braxton's grandmother Ethie would say, "all boy"—which meant constant adventures, fearlessness which led to countless bumps and scrapes, and occasional mischief. And, as God saw fit, the Stoneworth family tree had always bloomed with an abundance of male family members.

"Careful, Ace. You don't want to lose your dinner," Brandy warned as she stepped behind him and stopped the impromptu merry-go-round.

"Yes, ma'am," Ace said breathlessly. He clasped his hands together and sat as still as possible, which had to be torture for an eight-year-old.

After leaving his seat, Braxton found himself standing near the back of the room, in the space between the family room and the kitchen, near his youngest brother, West, and the family council of teenagers. Though West was twenty-five, he was still young enough to be accepted by that crew and often used the leverage to minister to them. Braxton knew this because that's what all Stoneworth men did; they passed along what they'd been taught through love, relationships, and their own example.

Braxton remembered what it was like to hear this family story as a teenager—after having heard it already dozens of times. He was tired of it. Wished someone would just write it in a book and give everyone a copy so they wouldn't have to keep going back to 1865 almost every time there were two Stoneworths gathered.

But now, at nearly thirty years old, Braxton appreciated his history. Not simply for what it meant to his blood kin, but for what a testament it was to God's faithfulness.

Braxton elbowed the leader of the teenage crew, Cayden, in the ribcage. As he watched the boy wince, Braxton teased, "Need to tighten up, boy."

"Man, I been lifting weights," he said, rubbing his chest. "Made varsity this year."

"Reals?"

"Yep. Dad says I'm better than Uncle Reth was in high school."

"Better than my dad?"

"Yep."

"I better get on your good side, then, 'cause you 'bout to blow up," Braxton teased, pulling his younger relative into a rough hug.

"Cut out all that talkin' back there," Uncle Bush ordered.

Braxton and Cayden straightened up immediately, wearing smirks that sent another round of laughter around the room.

But seriously, as Braxton watched the sparkle in Uncle Bush's eyes and listened to his rickety voice recount their family history from Emancipation through the 1900's, Braxton wondered if, some day, *he* might be the one to tell the story. He listened more intently now, making mental notes that he hoped would stick.

After his great-great-grandfather, Isaac, decided on a family name, he'd started his own church because their local pastor, Reverend Lupo, kicked Great-Great Grandpa Isaac out over a dispute regarding scriptures. Between Isaac and Reverend Lupo, only one of them could read. When Isaac volunteered to teach Rev. Lupo to read, he got angry and kicked him and Great-Great Grandmother

Evelina out.

So Great-Great Grandpa Isaac founded "The Trueway Church" in east Texas. Wasn't long before the church began to double as a funeral home, once the practice of embalming took off and the government started regulating what became an entire industry. Isaac's former slave owner's son, a man named Jed, gave him a lump sum from the estate and taught Isaac how to operate one of the first and by far most successful black-owned funeral homes in the 1900s.

As it turned out, funeral homes became big business in the south. Isaac passed the business down to his three sons, Cleo, Percy, and Jethro.

"Now, Percy was my granddaddy," Uncle Bush gleamed with pride.

Somehow, even the smallest children were still paying attention.

"He taught my daddy, Reid, the funeral business front to back. My other uncles and aunts didn't really want nothin' to do with dead bodies and such—"

"Ew! Dead bodies!" Lauren shrieked.

"Yep." Uncle Bush nodded. "Death is a part of life, young lady. You remember that. Nothing to be scared of if you switch lives with Jesus."

Lauren sat back again, apparently comforted by the alternative.

"Anyhow, when my granddaddy died, my Daddy got the business. He bought out his two brothers and two sisters' interest in the business. He got it all for himself. Lots of work, but he did it. That's one thing about the Stoneworths—we ain't afraid of hard work. When my uncles and aunts got their money, they worked hard, too. Got their schoolin', started their businesses—they didn't waste it, now. You hear me?"

Ace saluted. "Yes, sir!"

Brandy shook her head as though embarrassed, but the dimple in her cheek said she couldn't have been more proud of her outspoken son.

"Aaaaaaace!" Braxton's brother, Jarvis, encouraged the boy's attention-seeking behavior.

Brandy punched Jarvis's shoulder.

"Ace is one cool dude," Jarvis insisted. He shot Ace a thumb's up.

Ace returned it with a smile.

Jarvis was still a big kid, himself. Though he was only a year younger than Braxton, he played video games way too much and spent far more time posting and tagging on social media than any grown man probably should, in Braxton's opinion. And yet there was something comforting about the fact that Jarvis hadn't weighed himself down with a bunch of worries and responsibilities. Braxton and his four siblings, ranging in age from twenty-three to thirty, were all still decidedly young, enjoying the free space between young adult and full-fledged-grownup. At least for a little while longer.

Uncle Bush's voice lowered slightly as he recalled a rough time in the family, when he, Uncle Hiro, and Braxton's father, Reth, experienced a rift from their three brothers, Shiloh, Rule, and Pax, after Reid was no longer able to run the business. When the funeral industry began to decline, in the 1980s, they had a hard decision to make—one that tested their loyalties and their faith. Despite the temporary rift, selling the remaining land but keeping the mineral rights had proven to be the most profitable decision in the long run. In time, everyone came back together in forgiveness and love—and the checks were still flowing to this day.

"So you see, we got a long history of being there for one another. Everybody got to make their own decision about the Lord, but if you look back on the Stoneworths, you can see what the right choice is just by how good He's been to us."

By this point, Braxton was listening so intently, it was as though it was his first time hearing about his own family.

Silently, he prayed that he would never again do anything to bring shame on himself, his family, or his God.

Never again.

Chapter 2

Is this a school or an upscale mall? Tiffany Warren wondered as she parked her car in a visitor's spot and took in the massive red-bricked buildings with white trim built in a hollow of greenery that she imagined only existed at the late Michael Jackson's Neverland Ranch.

Red Sea Christian Academy's website didn't do them justice. Each edifice within view was clearly marked—Administration, Elementary, Junior High. She imagined the Senior High must have been one of the buildings nestled further back on the grounds. There was a maze of covered walkways between buildings, sending an unmistakable message: We didn't throw this charter school up overnight.

Tiffany took a deep breath, reminding herself why she had come. *Don't be skurd.* This was her domain. Organization. Business. Management. Though this school had all the appearances of a well-run establishment, there was more work to be done here. She'd found the ad for a contracted trainer online, read through their needs, and realized she was a perfect fit for the job. Their campus leaders needed help learning how to successfully manage people and projects to improve efficiency and student achievement. Her MBA along with the few undergrad classes she took in education, before she changed her major, would come in handy in helping her win the contract...or else she'd be eating Ramen noodles for the next several months.

She killed her car's engine and threw the keys into her purse. "Lord, be with me as I meet these people. I know there are other companies vying for this position, but You know I really, *really,* for *real,* for real need this contract." Then she remembered the teachings of her Sunday school teacher. Reluctantly, she added, "God, I submit to Your will, though. You know what's best for them and for me. Let it be so. In Jesus' name, Amen."

Hopefully, the Lord's will and her will were in sync—she did enjoy having electricity, water, and food.

Stepping out of her car, Tiffany headed toward the administration building with her laptop case in her right hand, her purse over the left shoulder. As she approached the building, she checked out her appearance. The gray pencil-skirt could have used another inch or two of fabric, but she realized this was an optical illusion. At five feet eleven inches tall and a hundred-fifty pounds, her legs always looked longer, leaner, and more "exposed" than they actually were. The heels added another three inches, putting her in the same stratosphere with most men, which wasn't so great for dating but went over well with playing basketball and conducting business meetings.

Tiffany tugged at the bottom of her fitted jacket, making it lay smooth and flat against her hips and stomach. She could have been a model—or so she'd been told—due to her height, naturally slim build, flawless skin and sharp features. But the idea of sitting in front of a camera all day never sat well with her. She was much too active and impatient, with little tolerance for divas and drama.

Her long back tresses blew in the crisp fall wind but settled as she came under the door's canopy. The automatic doors slid open and Tiffany found herself in the midst of an entrance fit for a king. Marble floors, shiny granite countertops, a chandelier shipped in from the movie Titanic. *Really? This is a K-12 school?* None of her colleges had been this nice, not even during homecoming week.

"Hello! I'm Rhonda. How may I serve you?" the receptionist, an older woman with a pair of horn-rimmed glasses asked. Her bronze-dusted hair sat in a loose bundle on top of her head.

"Hi. I'm Tiffany Warren. Here to see Mr. McDonald."

"He's finishing up with someone, but I will let him know that you're here."

"Thank you."

"May I scan your driver's license for security purposes? It's state law now."

"Sure," Tiffany said as she retrieved her ID from her wallet. *Times sure have changed.* She'd only been out of high school for ten years, and already we'd come to *this*?

The woman pushed Tiffany's license through a

small rectangular device, then gave it back.

"Thank you."

"No problem. You're welcome to have a seat—oh, wait!" She glanced down at her phone. "I think this may be him now."

Rhonda answered the phone. "Sure thing." She nodded toward Tiffany.

Tiffany smiled as her stomach began to knot. *No joke. This is it*. Like she'd done so many times before basketball games, Tiffany yanked her game face in place. She needed to make a good—no, an *excellent*—first impression on this man. Since quitting her job at the Langley Project Management Firm, Tiffany had been flying solo, doing little management projects here and there for small companies: audits, inventory management, workflow reorganization. But this contract with Red Sea Christian Academy would mean steady bread-and-butter for months. It would also mean she wasn't completely insane for stepping out on faith and starting her own business at the ripe old age of twenty-eight.

The receptionist pointed left. "When I buzz, you'll go all the way down the hallway. Take a left at the double-doors. Mr. McDonald's office is the last door on the left."

Tiffany nodded as she committed the directions to short-term memory.

Rhonda wasn't lying about going *all the way* down the hallway. It was quite a traipse, making

Tiffany wish she'd worn shorter heels. At the other end, she saw a man coming her way. Tall. Dark. Might be handsome, but he was still too far away to tell. *Mr. McDonald?* No. The website picture showed a gray-haired white man, much shorter.

And then she saw something else. Something small scrambling on the floor. Squeaking, running, it's little feet scraping on the tile.

The whole world went black as Tiffany's survival instincts kicked in gear. This thing was running toward her. Terror shot through her veins. She pressed the wall to her right for an outlet. Nothing.

"Sheeeek!" it screeched.

She screamed, too, intuitively searching for higher ground.

No stairs, no chairs, nothing in that hallway.

She found a door, pushed it open and ducked into the room just as the thing reached her ankle.

Still running off adrenaline, she kicked the thing. "Get back!"

"Whoa, whoa. It's okay," a male voice spoke.

The thing was being lifted off the ground by deep-brown hands.

Tiffany's heart tried to steady itself as she began to process the idea that danger had passed. *It* was being restrained now. Now that she could focus, she saw that *it* was a piglet.

She held a hand against her heart, trying to regain her composure while keeping her eyes on the beast.

"Tiff?"

She swallowed. *Did someone say my nickname?*
"Tiff."

Finally, she looked up into the face of the figure holding the pig. Another gush of energy shot through her. "Braxton?"

Maybe this isn't happening. Maybe the pig killed me and I'm in heaven now. But why would Braxton Stoneworth be here, too?

"Excuse me, sir," a child's voice interrupted her thoughts. "I'm sorry. My pig got away. Can I have it back?"

"Sure," Braxton transferred ownership to a little boy with a spiked-up mohawk.

The boy tucked the piglet under his arm. "I gotta take care of him for my agriculture class."

"Impressive," Braxton said as the boy walked away.

Braxton returned his attention to Tiffany. He reached for her hand. "You...want to step back into the hallway?" He pursed his lips. "I mean, you *are* in the men's restroom."

She glanced to the right and saw a row of urinals, confirming his claim. Tiffany shook her head. "I'm sorry. I..."

Gently, he grasped her hand, leading her back into the gender-neutral hallway. He picked up her laptop case from the floor and placed it in her grip. "Here."

She shook her head. "Thank you." Her breath returned. "I'm sorry. I don't—"

"Do animals," Braxton finished her sentence. "I

remember."

His face was coming into view now. Lean, angular facial bones, dark eyes fringed with thick lashes, a distinctly larger nose that somehow still worked with his squared chin and a mouth that she'd dreamed of kissing…a long time ago.

"Braxton. What are you doing here?"

"Fr…Sh…Um," he stuttered, "Tiff! I can't believe it's you! You're living here in Arlington now?"

"No. About a half-hour away, in DeSoto," she replied. "You?"

"Yeah, I'm in Arlington. North side. Near the lake," he said. For some reason, he wanted her to know exactly where he lived. Texas cities could be as large and wide as two or three smaller ones put together.

"That's good. And you're at this school because…" she left the question for him to answer.

"Just finished interviewing for a project management contract," he said. His gaze swiftly swept over her body, then settled on her face. "You look nice."

"Thank you." Tiffany smoothed her clothes in place again. "You look well, too." Quite the understatement, given Braxton's low-cut curly hair, perfectly set facial features and strong jawline. A second wave of emotion flashed through her, only this one wasn't the fight-or-flight reaction. It was the he-look-way-good effect.

Braxton asked, "What brings you to the Red Sea?"

"Apparently the same thing that brought you. The contract."

His eyebrows jumped. "You're in PM now?"

"Yeah."

"I thought your degree was in education."

"You thought wrong." *You've been wrong about a lot of stuff, buddy.* "I do have some background in education. But I've got my M-B-A. I think those two together put me in a great position for this job."

He touted, "That makes two of us with an M-B-A. Sounds like we'll be competing against each other."

"Yeah. Well, thanks for saving me from the pig. I've got to get to the interview now." She looked to her left. Right. The pig incident had thrown her sense of direction completely off. "Um...do you mind telling me how to get to Mr. McDonald's office?"

"Sure thing. But wait." He roughly patted her head.

She flinched. "Braxton, why are you touching me?"

"Because you just had a fight with a pig," he said.

Tiffany sighed. Had she not been so discombobulated, she might have laughed. Braxton always could make her laugh. "Oh." She took over the job, pressing her hair back in place. "Just point me toward his office."

He gave her directions and wished her well.

"Thanks."

"I hope we'll see more of each other this week," Braxton said with a glint in his eye.

Tiffany exhaled. "Maybe so. Have a good one."

What she hoped more than anything was that she'd get into this interview and blow Mr. McDonald away so he wouldn't even consider an extended interview with her competitors. She had to bring her A-game because she needed this job like Cheerios needed milk.

But the pig had thrown her off. So had Braxton. Tiffany giggled to herself, "That's one in the same."

Her sense of humor now in tact, she felt more confident as she twisted the knob to Mr. McDonald's office.

I got this.

Chapter 3

As Tiffany's backside swayed away from him, Braxton nearly pinched himself. *Did I really see Tiff Warren again?*

He wanted to call someone—his brothers, his father, his frats, anyone to tell them what had just happened. *Tiff Warren* was in the building. Under the same roof!

And she looked good, too. Even better than he remembered. Coffee-colored skin, high cheekbones and supple lips. Not to mention the new, sweetly rounded curves.

Back in the day, she'd had a girl-next-door charm with no makeup, a skinny body, and hair pulled back into a ponytail more often than not since she played basketball. Their first year of college, they'd met in an English class and become study partners, thanks to a project they'd been assigned to complete. Once the project was finished, they kept hanging out together. Watching movies in the lobby, sneaking food out of the cafeteria, making fun of short people. Before he knew it, they were friends.

When she invited him to the basketball banquet, Braxton had readily agreed since, obviously, there would be free food.

Tiffany had met him outside the dorm wearing an elegant red gown with her hair swept up and curls around her temples, all made up and wearing sparkling jewelry.

"You look…beautiful," he had told her breathlessly.

"Fool, it's just my prom dress from last year," she said, thumping him on the head. "Let's go get our grub on."

He still remembered the way she looked in that dress. Actually, "beautiful" had been an understatement. He'd wanted to smell her, caress her arm and pull her into an embrace in that moment. But she was adamant that they get there early to get the best seats and, possibly, the choicest entrees.

Of course, food was always a priority in college. He had walked alongside her that night as she jokingly linked her arm with his. He was wearing a denim button-down shirt, gray slacks, and athletic shoes. Since he wouldn't be called on stage, his attire was perfectly fine. Even if it hadn't been, he knew that Tiffany wouldn't have said anything. They were friends. Non-judgmental. Live and let live.

Only that night, he had wished to reclassify their relationship to something more.

That was right before the spring semester ended. All summer long, he'd called her and tried to go out, but they both had jobs—hers at a department store and his at the YMCA. It was hard to coordinate schedules. Not to mention the fact that neither of them had cars of their own. The thirty miles between his neighborhood in Dallas and hers in Garland might as well have been three hundred miles.

He couldn't wait to get back to school and see her that fall. Over the summer, he'd taken advantage of his job to lift weights. He'd put on twenty pounds, thanks to the protein shakes, too.

Tiffany had noticed the change right away when school resumed. He remembered the gleam in her eye as she ran a hand along his new and improved biceps. "Somebody's been working out this summer." It was the beginning of what he hoped would take them to the next level.

"A lil' bit," he had smiled as he flexed for her.

Things started heating up, slowly but definitely, over the next month.

But Tiffany wasn't the only one who spotted the change in Braxton. He also remembered the day Shawna Serrato had walked by and squeezed his arm. "Braxton, you got it goin' on! Might have to invite you as my special guest to the next Gamma Delta party."

Shawna Serrato touched me! The. Finest. Girl. At. The. Entire. School.

That was the beginning of the end of the beginning. He took Shawna up on that invitation and got an inside taste of Greek life on campus. Whatever he might have had with Tiffany quickly unraveled as Braxton became enamored with the idea of pledging a fraternity.

He joined the next line of Lambda Nu's and underwent ten weeks of what could only be described as hell on earth. Afterward, he wore the proud red and gold colors. Being a Lambda Nu at Pinkston College meant instant attention, popularity and power. And a whole lot of drinking.

Somewhere in that whirlwind of a semester, Tiffany quietly slipped out of his life.

But amazingly, today, she had slipped back in.

Walking back to his car, Braxton texted his father to let him know that the interview had gone well. He owed that much to his father. After all, Reth Stoneworth's name had earned Braxton more than enough favors over the years. A former professional football player turned well-known pastor, his father had influence in the Dallas Fort-Worth community, and Braxton wasn't too proud to throw around Reth's name when necessary.

This contract with Red Sea, however, would take more than a popular name. From the moment he'd met Jeff McDonald, Braxton could tell that the man was passionate about what he believed to be his God-given calling, to run an excellent school for the glory of God. Red Sea Academy's slogan, *Where God Does Amazing Things*, seemed to be more than just a lofty goal. It was the heart and soul of the school.

If Braxton got this contract, it *would* take a small miracle for him to meet their expectations. But he was a Lambda Nu man. Always up for a challenge.

Proud of you, son, his father's text read.

That was the second best news of the day.

Keep your head in the game, Tiffany reminded herself as she tried to focus on the words coming out of Mr. McDonald's mouth. Now that the interviewer had asked her all of his formal questions, he had encouraged Tiffany to ask her questions about the Red Sea Academy.

Mr. McDonald was answering her questions clearly, but all she'd been able to process so far were the various achievement plaques from the Texas Education Agency on the walls and the fact that the school, which had been in existence for eight years, took its Christian foundation seriously.

Since when is Braxton a Project Manager?

Tiffany glanced at the sentence she'd just typed on her laptop: *Five to seven teachers at each grade Braxton.* She quickly backspaced over the name and replaced it with the word "level".

"So, Ms. Warren, tell me a little about yourself." Mr. McDonald leaned forward and placed his palms on top of his cherrywood desk. The clock ticking above his head showed a good thirty minutes left in the time allotted for the interview. "What makes you the person for this job?"

This she could do without thinking. Tiffany snapped her laptop closed and cleared her throat in preparation for the branding-speech. "Certainly. The Warren Project Management was established—"

"No, no, no," Mr. McDonald cut her off. "I don't want the rehearsed, clinical, polished version of

Tiffany Warren. Tell me about *you*. Your passion, your goals, why *you* would be a good fit for the job."

He gave an encouraging smile.

Tiffany sighed. "Well, ever since I was a little girl, I've been a fixer. Math was my favorite subject in school because I'm a problem-solver. I also applied the skills to my family—whether it was repairing a broken doll or setting up a chore schedule for me and my sisters, I was the get-'er-done girl. Starting Warren Consulting was a bit unnatural, since it's quite a risk. But I'm enjoying it. And I think I'd like being around kids, too. They're so...energetic."

He nodded. "That's what I'm looking for. A genuine desire to serve."

"Good to know," she mimicked his bobbing head, thinking, *to serve and pay bills*.

"You mentioned a chore schedule. Tell me about it."

Mr. McDonald slid a sticky note from the stack and began scribbling.

"Well, I defined five major chores in our household: washing dishes, vacuuming, washing clothes, folding clothes and dusting. There were five people in the house, including my parents. Everyone had a job every week. We rotated so no one got stuck with something they abhorred. And since we all knew we'd end up doing each job, we gained an appreciation for how to make things easier on each other. For the most part, it worked out well."

He scribbled on for a few seconds longer, then

looked up at Tiffany and laughed, "I'm going to share this with my daughter. I think you just prevented world war three in her household."

Tiffany smiled. "Glad to help."

"Miss Warren, I'll be honest with you. We're looking at three companies for this contract. One's got a team of managers on staff. In fact..." he looked at my resume again, "your former employer, Langley."

"Mmm," Tiffany moaned to herself. *Wonder who they sent.*

"And then there's another small consulting firm that's not so much a PM company but is definitely headed by a man who, if he's anything like his father, is quite the charismatic team-builder. My concern for you is that this job may be more than what you can handle at this point in your start-up's growth. I mean, Warren Project Management is a one-woman-show, correct?"

She swallowed. "Yes, but I have a wealth of experience."

He raised a hand.

She stopped speaking.

"Don't worry. I will give it lots of consideration. And prayer. As should you.

"For the next three days, I'd like you to observe our campus. Tuesday with elementary, followed by a brief faculty meeting. Wednesday middle school and Friday with the high school. You'll visit our other buildings as well. It's only fair to pay you a reasonable fee for those days."

Tiffany's heart leapt. *Three paid days no matter what!*

He continued, "Even if you don't get the contract, we'd like your feedback from a business perspective. This is a school, but I recognized within my first few years as CEO that we can't accomplish everything we need to accomplish if we only work with those whose expertise lies K-12 education."

"I understand." *Where do I sign up for the free money?*

He handed her a paper with the terms outlined. Tiffany perused the page looking for the round figure and found it near the bottom, where she spotted a handsome daily rate along with a stipend for meals and travel. Though she had two pressing projects for other companies in the works already, Tiffany could hardly click the pen fast enough to ink this deal.

She pushed the signed page back to him.

He stood. "I pray that this experience will prove fruitful for you in one way or another."

Tiffany rose to her feet as well and shook his hand. "Thank you so much for this opportunity."

"See you in the morning. You might want to get here around seven-thirty. The before-school traffic can be daunting. Rhonda will have a schedule for you as well as a copy of our observation agreement."

"Perfect. I look forward to this."

"Same here." He gave a friendly wink. "Have a blessed day. And don't forget to pray."

Tiffany walked back down the hallway toward the main foyer thinking about what had just transpired: a feral pig, the distraction of Braxton, a warning about the competition. Her prayer list was growing longer by the minute.

Chapter 4

Tiffany returned to her apartment/office around noon and settled in for a long afternoon and evening of work. The Hillman project was turning out to be more than she imagined. Their bootleg inventory management system left too much room for human error. They were now at a point where they needed to decide whether to overhaul the system or retrain the employees. Tiffany had recommended a different inventory system more suited to their type of product, but the budget guys didn't see it happening any time soon. The whole thing was a mess at this point, yet they were making progress. Sometimes she had to mess things up before she could fix them. It was part of the process.

Her second project, with a homeless foundation in Dallas, was by far her favorite on the docket. They were compiling the stories of past service recipients for inclusion in a digital walk-through museum. Tiffany was coordinating the interviews, ghost writers, graphic designers, photographers and editors. For the most part, all she had to do was coordinate people's schedules, email follow up notes and facilitate communication between all the moving parts. She used special software to help keep up with everything.

In this case, the work sounded harder than it was.

Tiffany wasn't doing the work; she was only responsible for making sure the work got done. That's one thing she liked about project management: You got to hold people accountable. This made her the bad guy, at some level, but that connotation didn't bother her. She didn't know these people. She didn't have to relate to them on a personal level. This was business. And when the project was complete, she was out of there. Move on to the next one.

The Red Sea Christian Academy contract was projected to last ten months. The scope of it would take twenty hours a week, at least, and much of it would have to be accomplished face-to-face due to the nature of their work. Getting this project would push her to understand a new sector, but she was up to the challenge.

The week before her father passed away of a sudden heart attack, Tiffany had told him about her new company.

"You quit your job?" he had asked. Though he had tried to under-react, Tiffany still saw the trepidation in his soft, dark brown eyes.

"Yes, Daddy. Langley gave me good experience, but I can't stay there anymore. There's no room for growth. I don't get to go to any seminars, I barely know what's going on in my industry. Plus there's too much drama. I think I can do better on my own."

Then, the worry in the creases of his brow had smoothed away, almost magically, as her father said, "Yeah. You've always been good at figuring things, the science of math and the mystery of people. You got this, baby girl."

Her father's vote of confidence was still the only one that mattered.

For some reason, she wondered if Braxton's father was backing him, too. From what she recalled, Braxton had a close relationship with his family. His father had... like...six brothers and Braxton was the second of five children. Those Stoneworths definitely believed in reproducing.

They had high expectations due to a family history of success, which at first sounded braggadocios. But at the end of what was an almost unbelievable tale of his family's accomplishments, Braxton was clear about one thing: They owed all thanks to God.

Tiffany opened a browser on her laptop and googled Braxton Stoneworth. Up popped the results she was searching for. *Braxton-Gable-Stoneworth Business Consulting.* She smiled at the clever way Braxton had used his full name to make his business sound like a powerful company with multiple minds at work. Looked like he was trying to make a name for himself instead of riding his father's coattail.

She navigated to the website and clicked on the About page. There, she read that Braxton had earned a bachelor's degree a year after she earned hers, but an MBA soon thereafter.

Why did it take him so long to finish undergrad?

Tiffany scrolled down more to read the rest of his

bio. He'd won a few awards and given speeches at conferences. His past clients list was impressive for someone who hadn't been in business long. Granted, those older projects were mostly related to the sports world, but she couldn't fault him for using his father's network to get a start. He'd diversified his clientele with time.

The more she read, the more Tiffany realized that Braxton was indeed a formidable opponent in this race for the contract. *He might actually know what he's doing.*

A grin pulled at her lips as she remembered the old Braxton—the lanky boy from Falcon Hall— throwing rocks at her dorm window to get her attention. Though they had cell phones, the signal was weak at her dorm. He'd actually broken the cheap window one time. Tiffany covered for him, saying she wasn't exactly sure when or how it happened. When they billed her for the window, Braxton paid for it and thanked her profusely for keeping him from a vandalism charge.

Yep, she'd lied for him. After their first year, she'd also fallen for him.

But he hadn't caught her. He'd let her tumble all the way down, and then he'd stomped on her heart with those big red and gold Lambda Nu boots.

Tiffany shook her head and snapped back to reality. She closed the browser and maximized the windows pertaining to her current projects again. *Keep your head in the game.*

By five o'clock, Tiffany realized she needed a break away from the computer to breathe again. Her feet had begun to swell from being in one place too long and her contact lenses had become dry from staring at the computer screen without blinking. Plus she had to use the bathroom and eat something.

After taking care of her body's needs, she resumed work on the computer.

Her phone dinged with a text from her best friend since seventh grade, Cassie Abrams. *You still coming tonight, right?*

Tiffany couldn't remember what Cassie was talking about. She tapped the screen to open her calendar and saw a note she didn't even remember typing: *Plan Kanika's baby shower at Cassie house.* The time had been set for six-thirty to eight p.m.

"I don't have time for this," Tiffany whispered to herself. She texted Cassie asking if they could just do a virtual chat.

To which Cassie replied: *NO! We need to make food samples to see what will work best for the party. Hawaii. Remember?*

No, Tiffany didn't remember. Until just now. It was all coming back to her. They'd decided to have a Hawaiian-themed party as an inside joke since Tiffany and her husband were planning to name the baby boy after his grandfather, Hiawatha. They'd told Kanika about it and she thought it was hilarious. There was no turning back now.

Ok. I'll be there.

Cassie's townhome community had been using the same gate code for nearly two years now, which made Tiffany wonder why they even had a code. Exes, old tenants—anyone—could get through with 2287.

She pressed the buttons and waited for her friend to answer. "Yeah?"

"It's Tiff."

The automated system blared, "You may enter," as the iron gate opened.

Tiffany parked and headed toward Cassie's door. She suddenly wondered if she was supposed to bring anything. *Too late now*.

Cassie greeted her with a hug. "So glad you made it." She wore leopard print flats, black tights, and an oversized, red flannel shirt that could have doubled as a dress. As casual as the outfit appeared, Tiffany knew Cassie had probably spent hundreds of dollars for each piece in some swanky store. The girl had taste, which came in handy for her retail buyer's position with Michael Kohrs.

"I'm glad to be here, too," Tiffany dragged her words, though she meant them. Spending time with her friends had become a low priority for her, especially since she'd quit her full-time, steady-paying job. Tonight, she'd try to relax and catch up with her girls. Hopefully, no one would have any life-changing events for a while. That would give her enough time to establish the business and get herself together so she could give her friendships a little TLC.

"Monice and Tyra have already started on desserts. Did you bring any recipes?"

Tiffany gave Cassie the look of "duh."

Cassie made a popping sound with her full, high-gloss lips. "Yeah. I guess I forgot who I was talking to. Come on in. We'll let you wash dishes or something."

Monice, Cassie's cousin, was at the counter rolling something in a bed of coconut.

"Oh, no. I was gonna give you a hug, but I can't even look at a coconut." Tiffany blew Monice a kiss from the opposite counter.

Monice flipped her bangs back and scolded Tiffany. "You gotta try new stuff, Tiff. Expand your horizons. Grow up, girl!"

"Not if it means eating coconut. There's something wrong with the texture. I don't even think human beings are supposed to be eating them. Did you pray about it first?"

Her friends laughed at Tiff's sense of humor, which put her at ease and served as a subtle reminder of her real self. Not the business, do-what-I-say Tiffany, but Tiff—the 'round the way girl, who was invited to a cooking party despite the fact that she could hardly boil water.

Next for greetings was Tyra, who was mixing something up in a bowl.

"Hey, girl," Tiffany hugged Tyra from the side.

"Back atcha. Where you been anyway? Haven't heard from you in a minute."

"I been around. Workin' like a my middle name is Kizzy."

"Ha!" Tyra hollered. "Girl, I miss me some you!"

Tyra had also graduated from the same high school with Cassie and Tiffany. Though Cassie attended another university, Tyra and Tiffany had been roommates while at Pinkston their freshman year. Tyra had gotten pregnant, however, and moved back home. With the help of her family and friends, she had earned her degree, gotten a job in HR for the Dallas police department, and was doing quite well for herself and her daughter, Symone.

"Here. Taste this." Tyra held the whisk up.

Tiffany examined it visually, first. Then took a sniff of the yellow batter. "Does it have coconut in it?"

"Oh my gosh, Tiff!" Tyra gave up and ran her own finger along one of the metal wires. She licked her finger. "It's perfect." She threw the whisk in the sink. "Make yourself useful. Wash that off."

"Whatever," Tiffany fussed. "I'll wash when you guys finish. But I can't just eat something that I have no prior knowledge of. You could have frog legs in there for all I know!"

"Hey now," Monice jumped in with her New Orleans drawl, "don't make fun of frog legs 'til you've tried 'em. That's good eatin'."

Tiffany's stomach ached at the thought. She sat on a stool at the kitchen's island and watched as her friends carried on with the hard work of cooking. "I just can't get involved with stuff I haven't thoroughly examined."

"Now, see," Cassie said, opening the refrigerator, "that's why you're gonna be single for a mighty long time."

"Ooh!" rang through the kitchen.

Tiffany shot back, "Uh, hello! I don't see narry one of y'all with a man, either!"

Cassie set a tub of butter on the island and put a hand on her hip. She blinked rapidly at Tiffany. "Well, seeing as you've been all preoccupied with your new business, you wouldn't know, now would you?"

"What? You got a boo now?"

"I sure do," Cassie bragged.

Tiffany waited for the surprise outburst from Monice and Tyra, but their silence said it was true. And they already knew.

"What? Who is he?" Tiffany asked.

"A guy. From my job. The New York office."

"New York?" Tiffany repeated.

"Yep. He's very nice."

"And very white," Monice added.

"White?!"

"Yep," Cassie said, rolling out a sheet of puff pastry. "I can't wait forever for the brothers, you know."

Tiffany huffed, "We are not even thirty yet. We're not desperate."

"Speak for yourself on both counts," Monice said. "Besides, I wouldn't consider a white man a last resort. A man with no teeth, a man straight out the pen—yes. But white in and of itself, not a problem."

Cassie spilled the beans about the new man. His name was Charles. He was originally from Virginia. Graduated from the University of Michigan. Had done quite a bit of traveling with the company. The more Cassie spoke of him, the wider her smile grew. Tiffany could only be happy for her friend.

Tiffany gave herself a moment to digest this new information as she continued watching her friends consult one another about the food, mixed with conversation about Cassie's new Boo. *Needs more vanilla. Add salt. What church does he go to? No, you're making those patties too big.*

When they'd finished critiquing each other, Cassie called Tiffany to the sink. "Need you to get on these dishes, sis."

"Okay." Tiffany took her spot, busting suds.

"What's up with your love life these days," Tyra asked.

"Nothing. I don't have time for a love life," Tiffany said.

"You must have run across at least *one* man," Monice pried.

Tiffany admitted, "I did run *from* a man today."

"What?" they chorused.

"I was at this huge school. They've got all these programs to help the kids become well-rounded. Anyway, this one kid evidently had a pig. The pig got away and chased me down the hallway. And this guy rescued me."

"Was he nice?" Tyra asked.

"He was Braxton Stoneworth," Tiffany replied.

"Braxton Stoneworth?" Cassie and Tyra echoed simultaneously.

"Who's he?" from Monice.

"Oh my gosh, she was so in love with him," Tyra gushed.

"No, I—"

"Please. No lies," Cassie said.

"How would you know? You weren't even at the same school," Tiffany asked incredulously.

"Because he's all you talked about when we got together over breaks," Cassie recalled.

Tiffany pleaded with Monice. "Don't believe them!"

Monice laughed. "My name is Bennet and I ain't in it. I'm just listening.

"Let me tell the story because Tiff…Tiff was in total denial."

Tiffany stuck wet fingers in her ear. "La-la-la-la-a."

Her protests were met with Tyra's church-usher finger. "Hush."

Outnumbered, Tiffany could only lean against the sink and listen.

Tyra turned her back to Tiffany and addressed Monice and Cassie. "Here's what happened. Braxton Stoneworth, son of football great Reth Stoneworth, and Tiff were in-sep-ar-a-ble," she exaggerated. "And they kept telling everybody 'we're just friends'," she mocked in a childish tone.

"We *were* friends," Tiffany reiterated.

"So then...well, I can't really say exactly what happened after freshman year because I had to leave. But from what I understand, when Braxton pledged Lambda Nu, he lost his mind for a minute. He turned into the biggest dog on campus. Tiff dumped him with the quickness. She transferred. And from what I heard, when Braxton finally came to himself, was quite a broken-hearted prodigal boyfriend."

Shocked, Tiffany asked, "Says who?"

"People. As you'll recall, I was still stupid back then. Trying to keep up with Symone's dad. Keeping my ear to the grapevine," she admitted.

"So, here's my main question," Monice posed in a serious tone, "is he fine?"

"No," Tyra answered. "He was tall and rail-thin."

"But that was then," Monice fired at Tiffany. "Is he fine *now*?"

Tiffany shrugged innocently. "I don't know."

Unfazed, they fired questions at her like an automatic tennis ball machine: *Did you see a ring on his finger? Did he have any tattoos? Does he have brothers? Does he look like he has good credit? Was he wearing an ankle monitor?*

Tiffany yelled, "What in the world is wrong with you people?"

Cassie halted the madness, "Wait! Isn't his dad the Pastor at New Zion?"

"Yes, I think so," Tiffany guessed.

"They have Monday night service, streaming live. Let's go online and see if he's there. You know they usually sit the family up front."

Cassie retrieved her laptop from the sofa and set it on the island.

Tiffany complained, half-covering her face with her hand. "We were never together. And this was, like, nine or ten years ago."

They were all ignoring her.

A minute later, Pastor Reth Stoneworth was on screen preaching a sermon about how to meet the enemy at the gate. "The moment a thought arrives at the gate of your brain, meet it with the word. Close the door, my brothers and sisters."

"Amen," Cassie jumped in as all four women huddled around the screen.

I can't believe we're doing this.

"Well, the dad is fine. Hopefully, the apple didn't fall far from the tree," Monice whispered as though they were attending a sacred ceremony.

"There he is!" Tyra screamed, pointing at Braxton's tiny head on the fifteen-inch monitor.

"Enlarge it!" Monice ordered.

Cassie obeyed, using her fingers to operate the touch-screen function.

"How in the world did you let him get away?" Monice hollered at Tiffany. "He got any brothers?"

Absentmindedly, Tiffany replied, "A ton of them."

Monice slapped Tiffany's arm. "Hook us up!"

Tyra leaned toward the screen and mumbled, "I gotta admit—time has served brother Braxton well." She shivered dramatically.

Thankfully, the camera moved away from Braxton.

"Tiffany. Girl," Cassie said, shaking her head, "looks like you got a second chance."

"Who says I want a second chance with him?"

"Girl, if you don't, I'll take it," Monice said, squinting at the laptop again. "Sign me up for the jubilee, honey."

An unexpected, but unmistakable, twinge of jealousy twitched in Tiffany's chest. She closed Cassie's laptop.

Her friends screamed in protest.

"Can we please just get back to planning this baby shower? We haven't even discussed games, party favors…nothing!"

Cassie shook her head. Monice tsked and sighed.

Tyra laughed, "Okay. I see you, Miss I-do-not-nor-have-I-ever-had-feelings-for-Braxton-Stoneworth."

Tiffany rolled her eyes and reveled in the safety of standing over the sink, where she could hide the grin welling up inside her.

Braxton was heartbroken over me?

Chapter 5

Tiffany had gotten a grand total of five hours sleep Monday night. After hanging out at Cassie's, she had returned home to continue working, staying up so late she could hardly focus. When the charts on her screen wouldn't stop squiggling, Tiffany collapsed on her bed.

What seemed like a few hours later, her alarm clock announced the dawn of a new day. Dragging herself out of bed, Tiffany prayed that the classes she observed wouldn't bore her back to sleep. For insurance, she downed an energy drink just as she headed out the door.

The morning's traffic was less congested than she'd expected, which meant she arrived even earlier than planned.

Rhonda was waiting with the same bright smile. "Good morning, Ms. Warren."

"Good morning."

"Here's your visitor's badge and your class schedule, young lady. There's a map of the elementary building on the back side." She presented a yellow sheet of paper.

Tiffany smiled, taking the adhesive label and pressing it onto her white blouse. She took the yellow sheet from Rhonda as well. Her first class was kindergarten, Mr. Williams.

"You can wait in the teacher's lounge until the bell rings. Let me show you on the map."

Rhonda gave Tiffany a quick summary of the layout, circling the classrooms on her agenda, as well as the lounge.

"Thank you. Um...are there any...animals in the buildings...running loose?"

"No, not usually," Rhonda said, scratching her cheek.

Man up, Tiffany. "Okay. Thanks again."

Tiffany traveled along the paved path to the elementary building with its massive colonnade and scroll-like ornamental features. Inside, a second receptionist asked her to sign the guest log. Tiffany was the first entry for the day, which came as a slight relief. She was already ahead of her competition.

Tiffany followed the map to the lounge, which obviously doubled as a workroom. Several teachers were busy making copies, cutting out shapes on some contraption, and tearing off giant rectangles of colorful butcher paper. The atmosphere buzzed with creativity and excitement as they prepared for the day. Tiffany smiled at each teacher but stayed out of their way and friendly conversations, taking a seat on one of the couches against the wall of inspirational posters.

She powered her tablet and opened a new file, where she recorded her first observations. She noted the professionalism of the receptionists and the orderliness of the workspace. Similar to the human body, a company's health was often reflected in appearance and vigor.

Tiffany eyed the entrance as the door to the lounge opened again.

Oh no. Tiffany's shoulders flew back as Deja Robinson, her nemesis when she worked at Langley, walked into the room.

Deja briefly greeted the teachers, then threw a smug grin at Tiffany as she sat on the adjacent loveseat, slinging her curly extensions over her shoulder. "We meet again."

Tiffany didn't even attempt a smile. "Yep."

"I'm surprised you'd attempt to land a contract this large so soon," Deja said under her breath, her gaze leveled as low as an elderly woman looking above the rim of her glasses.

"Gotta start somewhere," Tiffany quipped.

Deja tilted her head sympathetically. "Well, don't worry. You'll get better with each proposal and then one day"—she clicked her cheek—"you'll land your first big contract. So this really is good practice for you."

Tiffany glared at her. "I'm not here to practice. I'm here to *play* and *win*."

"Girl, who are you kidding? It's me. *Deja.* I was in the next cubicle over. We worked on projects together. You and I both know you don't have the resources to pull this off," Deja hissed.

Tiffany kept her tone low and cool. "You don't know *what* I have."

"I'm not trying to sabotage you, Tiffany. But the last thing you want to do as a new company is overcommit and underperform," Deja warned.

Coming from anyone else, Tiffany might have heeded the advice. But Deja had it all wrong. Tiffany and Deja hardly worked anything "together". It was always Tiffany who'd worked on the cases and took up the slack that Deja dropped. Working with Deja was like doing the work of 1.75 people. The only reason Deja still had a position at Langley was because she made the company look good, literally, at presentations and in the local magazine articles. A dead ringer for Meagan Good, she had learned to use her looks and that phantom degree from an overseas-based online university to make her way in a male-dominated field.

If Langley got the contract, Deja certainly wouldn't be handling it. She had certain gifts of persuasion, but her work ethic lacked a pulse.

Tiffany concentrated her energy on taking notes again, ending the conversation with Deja by breaking eye contact. *The nerve of her!*

Tiffany calmed herself by praying, asking God to protect her mind from discouragement. With that prayer came compassion. Perhaps Deja believed every word she'd said. Maybe, in her mind, she *did* help Tiffany on those projects.

She decided to give Deja the benefit of a doubt. Tiffany looked at her former coworker again. "No matter what, I hope it goes well for whoever gets the deal. It's really about what's best for the kids."

"Please. Don't try to act nice now that you realize you're in over your head."

Okay. Shadow of doubt now dissolved.

A hush fell over the room. Tiffany glanced up from the screen again to see Braxton coming toward her. His pure male aura filled the room and his high-voltage smile sent a pleasant shock through Tiffany. Somehow, she was processing Braxton's handsome features all over again and more intensely now that she wasn't distracted.

"Hellllo," one of the teachers said to him.

"Good morning. Morning everyone," he spoke to the sudden fan club.

The teachers' voices morphed into high tweets as they acknowledged him.

Tiffany heard Deja grunt three times. "There is a God somewhere."

Braxton nodded at Deja while sitting next to Tiffany. He didn't wait for Deja's response before offering a personal greeting, "Morning, Tiff."

"Tiff?" Deja snarled as her neck popped back. "You two know each other?"

"Yeah," he answered for them both. "We attended Pinkston College together."

"Oh. Did y'all date?"

"No," Tiffany blurted. "We were just friends."

Deja's face pinched as she seemed to be dissecting Tiffany's response.

She eyed Braxton next. Her eyes widened and her

face lit up like a Christmas tree as she noticed something near his feet. "You're a Lambda?"

Braxton grinned and hiked up his pant leg to expose his red and gold socks. "Yeah. You pledged?"

How could she at a nonexistent online school?

"No. I thought about pledging Delta, though."

"You could pledge grad chapter," he suggested.

Deja's full smile reminded Tiffany of all those Lambda groupies who used to surround Braxton and his frats after parties. And Braxton wore that same gloaty pride across his chest as he engaged with Deja now.

Some things never changed. *Well, at least he's not wearing an ankle monitor.*

The bell rang and the teachers scrambled out of the lounge. Braxton, Tiffany, and Deja stood, grabbing their bags.

He asked Tiffany, "Where are you going first?"

"Kindergarten."

"I'm first grade with Miss Jetter."

"Me, too!" Deja offered.

"Cool."

Braxton took the liberty of glancing at the schedule in Tiffany's hand. "We've got the same class at 10:30 in third grade."

"Well, I guess I'll see you then." Tiffany said.

Deja stroked Braxton's arm and took a few steps toward the door. "Let's not be tardy for our first class."

He waved her off with his left hand.

Against her will, Tiffany noted the fact that he wasn't wearing a ring.

"I'll meet you there," he told Deja.

She bristled. Tossed the hair again. "Suit yourself." She sashayed out into the busy hallway.

Alone with Braxton, Tiffany felt her insides quiver, so she tried standing perfectly still and holding her breath when Braxton smiled at her again. Lambda Nu or not, there was no denying the fact that he had grown into a young man more attractive than most. An attractive man who wore amazing cologne that had begun to settle deep in her lungs.

Beyond his sensory appeal, there was a certain joy about Braxton that suddenly made Tiffany feel like a kid fresh out of high school again, back when she'd been the most optimistic eighteen-year-old in the world.

She watched as Braxton's mouth set itself to say something, yet no words came out the first or the second time. On the third try, he finally said, "Tiff, I just want you to know that I'm really, *really* glad to see you again."

"It has been a while," she managed to speak.

His forehead wrinkled. "But are you...*glad* to see me?"

The question hung in the air while Tiffany contemplated a response.

Braxton twisted his lips to one side, a gesture she remembered fondly from all the days and evenings they'd conversed about the important things in life:

their hopes and dreams, their families, their faith…and how they might be able to get into the volleyball game free. Tiffany had appreciated the fact that, contrary to her father's warnings, Braxton hadn't been "only after one thing" when they sat on the tailgate of his roommate's truck and shot the breeze while eating Oreos or Funyuns.

How could he have thrown it all away?

That's why she couldn't answer his question of whether or not she was glad to see him. If she said "yes," she'd seem desperate. She'd be letting him off the hook. But if she said "no," she'd sound bitter, like she hadn't moved on.

Tiffany settled on, "I don't know."

"That's fair," he shrugged.

Another bell rang.

Braxton looked at his watch. "That's the three-minute bell. We'd better get going."

Tiffany agreed and followed him out of the lounge, where they parted ways without another word.

Chapter 6

She followed the map to the kindergarten wing, where she'd expected to find hordes of five-year-olds running wild before the final bell.

Instead, she found Mr. Williams' class waiting single-file just outside his room. He was at the head of the line, underneath the sign bearing his name. He inspected the students' orderliness, Tiffany supposed. When the teacher failed to acknowledge her, Tiffany joined in at the end of the row because that seemed like the right thing to do.

"Jordan, get in the center of your tile," Mr. Williams ordered.

A girl who'd created a bulge in the line looked down at her feet and adjusted herself a little to the right. Tiffany double-checked her feet to make sure she was centered, too.

Except for the shuffle of shoes, jackets, and backpacks, the junction was quiet. Reminders of appropriate hallway behavior were posted low enough for the students to see them as they traveled to their classrooms. The Student-of-the-Week for the three kindergarten teachers' classrooms were prominently displayed on posters hanging from the ceiling beams. *How cute!*

"Let's enter the classroom quietly, put our belongings in our cubbies, and get started on the morning picture. Remember you can describe what you see or create a story about what you see." Mr. Williams instructed. He unlocked the door and allowed the children inside. He stood at an angle to observe both the classroom and the hallway.

When Tiffany reached him, she introduced herself.

"Yes, we've been expecting you," he said in a flat tone. "You can have a seat at the back kidney table." He pointed toward a table in the shape of just that—a kidney.

"Thank you," Tiffany said.

Mr. Williams didn't return the kindness. He simply closed the door behind them and went about his business as usual.

Tiffany hadn't been expecting such a cool welcome, but that didn't faze her. She was used to being treated like a tax collector. Actually, it made her job easier. She threw on her poker face and sat down in the adult's chair at the table. Well, she tried to sit at the table, but with her long legs and the short height of the kidney, there was a huge mis-match.

Another glance at Mr. Williams reminded her that he probably didn't have this problem. A short man who wore khakis as opposed to her slim skirt, he could pull it off much more easily on a daily basis.

She gave up on the table and decided to perch the laptop on her thighs instead of fooling with the table.

Several students had flashed snaggletoothed grins at Tiffany. One had even asked Mr. Williams if she was his girlfriend. His neck turned splotchy red as he replied, "No, children. This is Ms. Warren. She's here to observe me today. Just ignore her."

That was just all kinds of wrong! First of all, she wasn't there to observe him, per se. She was there to observe the system. Secondly, it was rude to tell kids to ignore an adult.

Keep your head in the game. You're here to do a job, not make friends or give home-training.

Tiffany gave Mr. Williams a blank stare so he would understand: *Man, I'm Willie Dale Warren's daughter. I ain't scared of you.*

Then she remembered: *Willie Dale Warren is dead.* Her heart sank with another wave of realization that her father was no longer there to protect her, give her pep-talks, infuse his wisdom when times got tough.

As she watched the kindergartners attempt to respond to the picture of a child swinging, Tiffany recalled the times her father would take her, Tina, and Terri Anne to the park. With three girls in three different seats, it was quite a juggle to keep each one going. Though they were each perfectly capable of propelling themselves on the swing, they would beg, "Push me! Push me, Daddy!" Somehow, Daddy's pushes seemed to take them higher than their own attempts to keep the momentum.

One time, Tiffany had secretly counted how many times Daddy pushed her versus Tina and Terri Anne. That night, when he had tucked her in bed, she'd beckoned for him to come close so that Tina and Terri Anne couldn't hear. She whispered in his ear, "Daddy, I know you pushed me more today at the park."

He grunted, "Oh?"

"Mmm hmmm. You pushed Tina twenty times, Terri Anne twenty-three times, and me twenty-seven times."

Daddy tapped Tiffany's nose. "You sure are good with numbers."

She smiled up at his big, round face.

Then he winked at her and said, "Let's keep that secret between us, all right baby girl?"

"Okay," she'd agreed as the warmth of her father's love trickled from the tip of her nose to the depths of her five-year-old heart.

She wondered now how many of the little girls in this classroom were making life-long memories with their daddies. *God, I hope they have great dads, too.*

Blinking back tears, Tiffany wondered how much longer she'd have to ride out these tides of grief that overtook her without warning. It had only been four months since her father passed, but she was tired of the unpredictable surges already.

The morning announcements were a welcome distraction. Tiffany rose to recite pledges to the American flag and the Texas flag, followed by a moment of silence. She recognized Mr. McDonald's voice and took comfort in the fact that he was a father who still looked out for his daughter, although that daughter was an adult with children of her own.

He led the entire school in a prayer, and then the children along with Mr. Williams spoke an affirmation. "Mind is sharp, I am smart, my teachers are geniuses who love me with all their hearts. With God's help, today will be a great day. And even if it seems bad, I will remain grateful."

Tiffany didn't have any kids, but if she ever had any, she knew already she'd want them to attend Red Sea Christian Academy. Maybe not Mr. Williams's class, but any school that invited the Lord into every class was one that had to succeed.

As soon as Mr. Williams began the lessons, Tiffany got lost in the buzz of the children in the room. They were bright, inquisitive, articulate little people—way smarter than she remembered being at their age. She noted how Mr. Williams redirected off-task behavior politely and showed the students exactly how to write a story using letters they knew. "Don't worry if it's not perfect the first time," he told them with a comforting tone, "we can fix it later."

By the conclusion of class, Tiffany had changed her mind about Mr. Williams. He might not have been the friendliest dude, but he loved his students and taught them well.

Tiffany left his room at 10:25, as the students were transitioning into math time. Mr. Williams gave a quick nod and returned his attention to the children.

Stopping by the restroom, Tiffany checked her hair. Makeup. Clothes. She made her way to the third grade hall, where Braxton motioned toward a seat he had obviously saved for her in the back of the room.

This teacher, Miss Hopewell, introduced the children and had them say "hello." Braxton and Tiffany acknowledged them in return.

As much as she tried to listen and take notes, Tiffany became distracted by Braxton's presence. She tried to resurrect the image of the tall scrawny boy she'd met her freshman year. Nothing to write home about except he was hilarious. The man sitting next to her now, though...if he hadn't messed over her before, he could definitely have a chance after Tiffany landed the contract.

Thankfully, Miss Hopewell told Tiffany and Braxton that she'd put them to work if they wouldn't mind. They both agreed, and before she knew it, Tiffany was on her knees beside a soft-spoken girl's desk, helping her with fractions. "Okay, it's like this," Tiffany started to explain. "Wait...you have an extra piece of paper?"

"Yes." The girl tore a sheet from a spiral.

"Okay, this piece of paper is a whole sheet. One. If I tear it in half"—she demonstrated—"there are two parts to this one sheet. Right?"

She nodded.

As Tiffany continued with the demonstration, she witnessed first-hand the priceless moment the child finally understood the concept of parts to a whole.

"Oh. That's what it is?" she whispered in amazement.

"Yep. You got it." Tiffany winked.

A blazing smile screamed what the girl barely verbalized, "Thank you."

Standing to her feet, satisfaction flooding through her veins, Tiffany turned to find her next prodigy. There were no hands in the air. Sadly, she returned to her chair at the back of the room.

Braxton was helping a boy with his work. Tiffany looked on, noticing Braxton's animated approach to teaching. She raised up enough to see that Braxton had drawn a pie on a sheet of paper with a green crayon.

Within minutes, Braxton was high-fiving the boy, congratulating him on a job well done.

Miss Hopewell called everyone's attention. "Boys and girls, it's time to prepare for lunch."

Braxton joined Tiffany again in their area. "How'd it go?"

"Good."

"Same for me," he said. "But I have to admit that I've had practice teaching fractions."

"Really? When?"

"To my daughter. She was in third grade last year."

Tiffany's throat thickened. *Braxton's got a kid?* "Oh. You have a daughter? Are you married?"

"No, no. I'm single. Never married. My wild Lambda Nu days caught up with me," he admitted.

"Don't remind me," slipped from Tiffany's lips. She covered her mouth. "I'm sorry. I mean, I believe every child is a blessing from God."

"Agreed."

Miss Hopewell interrupted the conversation by nearing the table. "Lunch will be half an hour. The food in the cafeteria is decent."

"Thank you," Tiffany said, gathering her bags. "It was a pleasure being in your class."

Braxton stood with her. "Absolutely."

"Thanks for coming," Miss Hopewell said. "We could really use some help making sure we're all on the same page. Good luck to both of you."

Her attitude was certainly much better than Mr. Williams's.

Miss Hopewell instructed her pupils to say goodbye and thank Tiffany and Braxton for their help. As they were leaving, the little girl whom Tiffany had helped ran up to her side and threw her arms around Tiffany's waist. "You saved my life!"

"Awwww, you're welcome," Tiffany said, patting the girl's shoulder.

"Alright, Kelly, return to your seat." The girl obeyed as Miss Hopewell gave Tiffany an apologetic expression.

"It's okay," Tiffany said.

Braxton held the door as they entered the empty hallway.

Her high heels clicked authoritatively along the tile while the low thud of Braxton's shoes brought in the base.

"You're still quite a teacher. I remember when

you tutored me in Algebra. I got an A both semesters, thanks to you," Braxton reminisced.

"You earned them fair and square."

They passed an assembly of students taking a bathroom break. Their teacher, a heavy-built older woman with a Hawaiian print top and skirt, didn't speak.

Tiffany and Braxton ventured on to the cafetorium, where they stopped upon entrance when they realized that one of the kids was on stage with a microphone leading a prayer to bless the food.

After the "Amen", she and Braxton jumped in line behind a clump of students who seemed to be taking advantage of the opportunity to chat and relax a bit. A traffic light sat atop a stand on the stage. The green light was lit, for some reason.

Braxton closed in the space between them and whispered into Tiffany's ear, "Do you get the feeling that some of these people don't want us here?"

The depth of his voice and the sweet brush of his breath against her ear sent a tingle through her body. She swallowed. "Yeah." *Don't do that again.*

Tiffany moved her purse to rest on her hip so Braxton couldn't sneak up on her again. They passed through the food line ordering staple cheeseburgers and tater tots. Mr. McDonald had said they needed to experience the school, so Braxton thought it best that they sit at one of the tables in the student cafeteria.

Tiffany agreed because she didn't want Braxton getting an edge. "Works for me."

"Man, they got these kids trained," Braxton said under his breath.

They sat at the end of a table across from one another and a few seats away from any kids.

"How was kindergarten?" he asked.

"Fine. The kids were great. The teacher was a little reserved, but that's to be expected under the circumstances, I think," Tiffany explained. "How was first grade?" As long as she kept this conversation professional, there was no chance she'd get lost in Braxton's beauty and start fumbling over her words.

"I have no clue. Deja talked to me the whole time."

Tiffany laughed. "Really?"

"Pssssh. I thought the teacher was gonna give us detention."

A deeper laugh came from Tiffany now that his sense of humor had calmed her a bit. "You're still goofy, Braxton."

"If I recall correctly, I wasn't the only one with quick wit...*back in the day*."

The cafeteria grew louder as more children entered to eat lunch.

Tiffany raised an eyebrow. "I still have a sense of humor."

"I can't tell. I haven't seen anything but hard core, straight up diary-of-a-mad-black-woman outta you since yesterday."

She stifled her giggle. "I'm here on business."

He made the time-out sign with his hands. "Can

we take a break now?"

Tiffany gave a reserved sigh. "I suppose." *But I can't keep looking at you without getting jittery.*

"If you're saying words like 'suppose', you're not on break," he challenged.

"Okay, I'm on *for real* break. Now what?"

"Why did you leave Pinkston?"

Whoa. He didn't waste any time. Tiffany raised her shoulders, lowered them. "It was just time for a change." She bit into her burger.

"I thought about it. Yesterday. When I saw you."

"Thought about what?"

"About why you might have left. Without telling me. Without looking back."

Tiffany urged, "And?"

He ate a tater tot. Hesitated. "I don't want to assume anything."

"Good. You shouldn't. People transfer schools all the time."

"Not without telling their best friends," he stated.

Tiffany's eyes fell to the burger on her Styrofoam plate. *Best friend.* He was right. Braxton had been the closest thing to a best friend that year since Cassie had gone to a different school. His admission only made the sting of his rejection hurt all the more.

"Braxton, let's leave the past in the past."

"Hear me out," he insisted with pleading eyes. "Who knows—we're in the same field. We may have to work on a project together one of these days. Let's clear the air."

She rested her chin on a palm. "Go."

Braxton scooted his tray to the side and drew an invisible line on the table with an index finger. "Here's the chronology—"

"Chronology is a big word for somebody off the clock," she teased him.

"Touche," he gave a flirty smile. "Let me break this here down for you. How's that?"

Tiffany let another laugh escape as Braxton continued, "Fall semester. You and I meet. Become friends." He moved his finger over an inch. "Spring semester. Friendship continues." A quarter of an inch. "And then something happened."

Tiffany asked, "What?"

His eyes glowed with excitement, but just as he began to speak, one of the adults monitoring the room switched the light from green to yellow. Instantly the volume lowered as the children heeded the warning, converting their conversations to whispers.

Braxton leaned in and said, "You remember the spring basketball banquet? When you invited me to go with you?"

Tiffany leaned in. "Yes."

In a low hum, he continued, "And you wore that red dress, had your hair together, makeup on?"

Tiffany vaguely recalled that evening. "Okay?"

He marked the imaginary timeline again. "That's what happened. At least to *me*, anyway."

"What are you talking about?"

"I didn't want to be your friend anymore after that

night."

Tiffany frowned. "I don't understand. *I* thought you didn't want to be friends anymore because you'd found new ones in Lambda Nu—not to mention all the little-sister groupies and the frat activities taking up your time."

"No, no. That's not what I meant. I didn't want to be your friend anymore because I wanted to be *more* than friends," he clarified.

"You sure had a funny way of showing it," Tiffany retorted.

A succession of emotions flitted across Braxton's face as he processed Tiffany's words. "So...you thought I'd kicked you to the curb for Lambda Nu?"

"Yep. That's *my* version of the chronology." Tiffany wiped her mouth with her napkin and threw it on the burger. She wasn't hungry anymore.

"I thought we were on break?"

"Break time is over," Tiffany declared as quietly as possible with the yellow light still in force. She pointed toward a group of kids who were emptying their trays in big gray trashcans. "Looks like we dispose of our trash over there."

"Before I clock in, let me say for the record: I did not end our friendship for Lambda Nu."

"How can you deny it when that's exactly what happened?" Tiffany hadn't meant to get sucked into this conversation, but apparently Braxton had already begun the grisly task of exhuming buried memories.

"May I finish the timeline, please?"

67

"Go ahead," Tiffany acquiesced.

He drew the next segment. "Summer after our freshman year. I called you. Every day. We talked. Laughed. I thought we were going somewhere."

"So did I." Tiffany reached across the table and added on to where he'd left off. "Fall sophomore year, you pledge Lambda Nu." Inch. "Winter break-nothing." Inch. "Spring, you're drunk every weekend and some weekdays. You're dating Sue King, Leslie Grambs, *and* Virgie Odell. Meanwhile, I'm getting calls from university coaches who want me to transfer. So I leave. End of story." She dabbed an invisible period at the end of the table.

Tiffany noticed her shaking hand. She quickly tucked it under the table. *Why did I let him take me there?* Even more disconcerting was the fact that "there" existed. Tiffany rose to empty her tray.

Braxton followed closely, throwing away his unfinished food as well.

With the gentle brush of his hand against hers, Tiffany froze just outside the cafetorium.

She set her face like flint, willing her lips to stop quivering as she allowed him this moment in a quiet nook of the hallway.

"I'm sorry, Tiff. I guess I never really saw it through your eyes. All this time, I thought *I* was the victim."

"Braxton, there is no victim. It happened. It's over. We were, what, nineteen? Twenty? Kids." She tried to make light of the conversation with a slight chuckle. The chuckle, however, sailed out of her mouth as a high-pitched squeak instead.

Tiffany had never been so glad to hear a bell ring in her life. She turned on her heel, leaving Braxton in a pool of his own regrets.

Chapter 7

Braxton replayed the conversation with Tiffany in his brain all afternoon. While he was supposed to be focusing on a fourth grade teacher's science experiment, his mind was stuck on the history lesson Tiffany had given him.

She hadn't allowed Braxton the opportunity to finish his version of their demise. He was going to say that once he pledged, Tiffany stopped talking to him.

The big brothers had warned them that once they crossed over, they would have instant haters. Non-Greeks who wanted to pledge but didn't have the money or the guts, feminists who despised the fraternity's reputation, girlfriends who didn't understand the commitment they had made, old friends who felt left out. He thought that Tiffany had fallen into one of the last two categories. Her version was very different from his.

But would she listen to him? Did his account of events matter? In his experience with women, once they painted a picture of what happened and the paint dried, there was no redrawing the memory. The anger peeking past her exterior told him that there was no way he could rewrite history for Tiffany.

He was going to have to start from scratch...if he wanted to pick up where he'd left off, but did that even make sense? How could he pick up where he left off without addressing the discrepancies of their past?

As he paused once again during the futile attempt to take professional notes in the classroom, Braxton allowed himself to think through the question that had plagued him for the last nine years: *What could have happened between the two of us?* He'd always pushed the question away because, despite the worldwide web and social media, he had never been able to virtually stalk Tiffany. He saw her face here and there on a throwback post from college friends, but otherwise, she seemed to have fallen off the earth.

Seeing Tiffany's face again had changed everything, though. Granted, she had been running from a teeny tiny pig. And, since then, she had given him the cold shoulder for the most part.

Still. This was his chance to get an answer to questions he'd mused about for nearly a decade.

The last bell rang, leaving Braxton with a sinking feeling. He'd allowed this situation with Tiffany—if that's what he called it—to interfere with work. Woman-issues aside, he had bills to pay, child support to stay current on, and a personal obligation to himself: Don't let his father down again. The opportunity to compete for this contract had come thanks to one of his Dad's connections. An avid football fan, Mr. McDonald ran in some of the same circles with the senior Reth Stoneworth. With the exchange of a few handshakes and business cards, this possibility had landed in his lap despite Junior's recent mess-up that threatened to stain the Stoneworth name.

The Red Sea contract wasn't just about the work and the money; it was about getting back on track, catching on to a branch to interrupt a downward spiral. All his life, he had heard people say that sometimes you had to hit rock-bottom before you got a clue. Braxton couldn't find any scriptures to support that theory. He'd come close enough to rock-bottom to know he didn't want to see it. Ever. And this contract would give him the bounce-back he needed to propel himself to the top again.

As he exited the elementary building and walked back to the administrative building to briefly attend the weekly faculty meeting, Braxton silently prayed. *God, I can't afford to botch this proposal. Too much at stake. Keep me focused.* He considered praying about Tiffany, but what could he say? The whole thing was confusing.

With no idea what to ask for, Braxton simply ended the prayer, "In Jesus's name, Amen."

Deja had saved a seat for him between herself and Jeff McDonald at the front table of the grand meeting room.

"Oh. Thank you." Braxton reluctantly sat in the unrequested reserved seat. He didn't want to make a scene or let on to Mr. McDonald that there might be tension already.

When Tiffany entered, she was forced to sit on the other side of Mr. McDonald. Her nod to Braxton and

Deja was minimal, but she gave a hearty smile to Jeff, which was to be expected given his role.

The round tables in the room quickly filled with teachers, and the meeting opened with prayer. Rhonda introduced Braxton, Deja, and Tiffany as guests who were vying for the PM service that had previously been discussed with the faculty. A round of applause broke out, though Braxton could see that some people were more genuine than others.

He couldn't blame them. Some people viewed project managers with the same disdain as dentists, yet they wanted to sport all thirty-two teeth proudly. Can't have change, improvement, or even maintenance without some degree of discomfort.

Mr. McDonald thanked them all for hanging behind for a few minutes. "I just wanted them to know who you were when they see you in the hallways."

Braxton and his competitors thanked him and then left the room, escorted by Rhonda back to the main foyer.

"I look forward to seeing you again tomorrow," she said. "Stop by here first to pick up your route."

"Sure thing," Deja answered for the group. She led the way to the exit, followed by Tiffany and Braxton.

Outside, the wind rushed into their faces, a fresh welcome into the afternoon, away from work.

Deja commented, "Beautiful day."

"We can agree on that much," Tiffany said,

pulling her phone from her purse. She stopped as she dialed. "I'll see you guys tomorrow."

"Bye," Deja said, slowing her pace so that she could walk with Braxton to their cars.

He looked back at Tiffany, wanting to say something…anything, but she already had the phone to her ear.

He walked to the visitor's parking spaces with Deja at his side.

"How was your day?" she asked.

"Pretty good." *Except I couldn't stop thinking about Tiff.* "Yours?"

"Excellente," she cried with a fake Spanish accent. "But all those little kids? Whew—I could use a drink. What do you say?"

Braxton declined with a shake of the head. "Naaw. Gotta pass on that."

Deja's mouth fell open. "You're Lambda Nu. And you're passing on alcohol?"

He tilted his head respectfully.

"I've never heard of a Lambda who didn't drink. I need to see the brand on your chest for myself," she laughed seductively.

Braxton opened the door to his Lexus sedan. "You'll have to take my word for it. See you tomorrow."

He breathed a sigh of relief when Deja got into her car and left the premises. *Thank you, God.* As fine as Deja might be, she was getting on his nerves already.

74

He'd had his fair share of emotionally high-maintenance women. Could spot them a mile away. No matter what you did, it was never enough with that type. Too much drama. And most of the time, those women had two entirely different looks: one for catching a man and another for after-the-catch. He and his frats called it the Saturday-morning-laundry-girl-syndrome, when sisters just said "whatever" and went about the day looking like bad mug shots. Braxton understood the concept of dressing down, but he felt a woman should at least *resemble* the person who showed up for the first impression.

Tiffany, on the other hand, had flipped the script on him. Her Saturday-morning look was the same as her weekday look. It was only after she got all dressed up...

He glanced back at the administration building and saw Tiffany still standing at the entrance, engaged in an animated conversation. He lowered his window slightly. *Is something wrong?*

Braxton was in no rush. He waited for her to finish, then met her at the curb of the lot. Her face was contorted by either anger or sadness. He couldn't be sure. "You all right?"

"Yeah," she said, not looking at him, walking ahead.

Braxton double-timed to keep stride.

She pressed her key fob, causing lights to flash on an older model Chevy Impala.

"Nice ride," he complimented.

Tiff stopped suddenly and squared up with him. "Braxton, what do you want?"

"I...really don't know," he admitted. "I'd like to have a chance to figure out what I want."

She chuckled with annoyance. "It's always about you and what you want, isn't it? Typical."

"No. Look. If your day was anything like mine, you had a hard time concentrating on this project."

Her features softened a bit, telling him he'd spoken her truth, too.

"I think if either one of us wants to be at our best, we're going to have to call a truce, call Dr. Phil, call *somebody*, " he said.

Tiffany lowered her head, but not before he saw the break in her poker face.

He continued, "'Cause I couldn't stop thinking about...it...today." He realized he probably should have said the word "you" or "us" instead, but he wasn't going out like that if Tiff was dead set on dogging him.

"Fine. Truce."

"Dinner?"

"What?" she quipped sharply.

"Dinner. Tonight. You gotta eat when you're on a truce. It's one of the rules of war."

She blinked slowly, which was slightly better than an eye roll. "I am not at war with you. And I don't mix my professional life with my personal life. That's a rule of business."

"Uh huh." Braxton looked up to the heavens, as

though the thin clouds against the blue sky might yield a strategy to get Tiffany to agree to dinner. "Okay. Here's another rule of business *and* war." He pumped his eyebrows up and down. "Get this. You can't do what you have to do on an empty stomach."

Tiffany laughed, "That is *so* lame."

"Come on, Tiff, you're killing me here!"

She threw her head back. "Oh my gosh, Braxton, give me one good *real* reason why I should go out with you."

He was breaking her down with humor. *Yes!*

But the serious air that settled on her quickly dissipated his attempts to sidestep her concerns. He had to answer from the heart. "One *real* reason is…we were friends. Once upon a time."

Tiffany pursed her lips. "This is true. We were." She bit her bottom lip. "And I *am* hungry."

Chapter 8

Tiffany had hidden her disappointment when he'd suggested Maxine's Chicken. It was one of those over-hyped restaurants that served two or three items on the menu. Nonetheless, she didn't want him to think that she was overly concerned about this meal. To do so might get his hopes up much higher than she wanted them to be. The way he looked at her—eyes nearly shut from smiling—she knew Peaches & Herb's *Reunited* was crooning on the playlist in his head.

But she wasn't up for a reunion. He'd already burned her once. She'd be a fool to let him do it again. A friendship was all she might be willing to offer. It would be hard, though, given Braxton's attractiveness. And that cologne. Plus his sense of humor, disarming her when she least expected it.

"Just two?" the host asked.

"Yes," Tiffany replied.

They were led to a wooden table with half the varnish rubbed off. It could have come from her grandmother's house, really. Of the four chairs at their table, only two matched. Tiffany imagined that the owners had purchased the furniture at various garage sales and antique stores. An ingenious plan, actually, that added to the "right at home" feel.

She was glad she'd listened to Braxton now. A

stuffy restaurant with candles and linen napkins wouldn't have been right for this casual occasion.

The host explained how the restaurant worked. The two sides—French fries and green beans—as well as biscuits would be served family style and could be refilled as many times as they wanted without an additional charge. For meat, they had a choice of fried, baked, grilled or Bar-B-Q chicken.

"Thank you," Tiffany said.

When their waitress, a twenty-something who looked like she'd been at the top of a cheerleading pyramid, asked Braxton what kind of meat he wanted, he said, "I'll have the chicken."

To which the girl giggled uncontrollably.

Here we go again.

Tiffany interrupted their flirting. "I'll have baked chicken."

"Same for me."

Miss Pom-Pom walked away.

"What gives?" Braxton asked.

Tiffany shook her head. "What are you talking about?"

"Your attitude. It got stank when old girl came to take our order."

Tiffany laughed. "You know, it gets kind of old watching these women go goo-goo-ga-ga over you."

"You should join the club." He pointed at her. "I could make you president. Take you places, girl."

"Whatever!"

He cocked his head to the right. "All jokes aside.

What's really going on with you. I mean, one minute you cheesin', ready to go eat dinner with me. You claim you don't want all this." He put a hand on his chest. "But the minute another woman flirts with me, you got a problem."

Tiffany wished he weren't telling the truth, but he was. The gospel truth. She exhaled. "All of this reminds me of college. Not memories I want to relive."

"Has anything happened to you since then?" Braxton asked.

"Anything like what?"

"Other relationships. I mean, you can't be *this* mad over something that happened almost a decade ago."

Tiffany smacked, "Nope. Nobody else has dumped me except you."

"Awwww, snap! You didn't have to say it like that."

"It's the truth."

"So you haven't had a good friend or a semi-boyfriend since we were in college?"

"Nope."

Braxton peered into her eyes. Curiosity and wonder filled his gaze. "So, you're saying...you're still a..."

"Oh my gosh, are you seriously asking me about my sex life?" Tiffany fussed.

"I'm sorry. I didn't mean to get all in your business. Just trying to understand."

"Look. I'm a woman of God first, which excludes me from a lot of relationships. Secondly, I've been too busy working and growing professionally and spiritually to get romantically involved with anyone. Hope that answers your question."

Still wearing that awe-struck look, Braxton barely breathed, "Yeah. I get it."

The waitress provided a brief reprieve from Braxton's penetrating eyes. Tiffany could have kicked herself for telling him about her squeaky clean past. Of course, it was nothing to be ashamed of. She had made a commitment to remain pure until getting married, but did Braxton need to know that? Probably not.

Back in her early twenties, when there were still a few virgins left on the radar, she'd seen that gleam in a man's eye whenever they made it to the "tell me about your past" conversation. As soon as they got a hint of her purity, it was as though she was fresh meat thrown to the wolves. Even "church guys" wanted a piece of her without a ring. A conquest. A trophy.

As she entered her mid-twenties, it was basically understood that everyone had "done it" by then. Or else they were ugly as homemade sin.

And yet, when she'd told Braxton just now, he didn't quite have the mad-dog look in his eyes. It was more like he'd realized something remarkable.

Braxton opened his hands to her. "Pray?"

"Yes." She allowed his strong hands to envelop hers, wondering if her own hormones could be trusted any more than Braxton's.

"Father, thank You for this meal. Thank You for the hands that prepared it and served it. And thank You for the hands in my own right now. In Jesus's name, Amen."

"Amen."

She'd never been so grateful for a prayer to end. The heat from his palms seemed to radiate all the way up her arms.

After taking a bite of her food, Tiffany turned the tables. "So what have you been up to with relationships?"

He whistled sharply. "Too much drama."

"Are you the source of the drama?"

"Hmmm. Since you put it that way, probably. I mean, my parents have been married almost forty years. I know what a good relationship is supposed to look like. But somehow, I keep ending up in bad ones. With psychos."

"Not nice," Tiffany scolded.

"I'm just saying. When you follow a brother to his grandmomma's house and break in the back door—you crazy."

"You're kidding."

"I wish I were. My grandmomma nearly capped the girl with a sawed-off shotgun. Thought she was a burglar." He gave a fake frown. "And she was…trying to steal my heart and all."

Tiffany pretended to gag herself. "Who falls for this I'm-the-man act of yours?

He exclaimed, "Women everywhere! You just admitted it five minutes ago."

"Okay, but you just said all you attract is psychos," she countered him. "Why don't you just be yourself?"

"I *am* being myself."

"No, you're not," Tiffany said. "The Braxton I remember was humble. Genuinely interested in others. Sincere. Funny, but still a great listener.

"You remember when my phone got stolen from the chapel?"

"How could I forget. The irony."

"You let me use your phone for a whole week. I'd call home, talk to my parents, my sisters, or my friends. And when I got off the phone with them, you'd ask how everybody was doing. I must have talked forever about what was said which, in retrospect, was a bunch of nothing. But you listened. You even asked me if my Aunt Janie had her baby yet, which was something I'd actually forgotten to ask my mother. It was as though you cared about me, my family, and my conversations with these people you'd never even met. That's the Braxton I enjoyed most. Before Lambda Nu."

The overconfident smirk slipped from his face. "You don't think I'm still that person today?"

Tiffany dropped her fork and searched the windows to his soul for a trace of the old Braxton. His eyes were still as soft and endearing. The crease under them still eager. She confessed, "Yeah. The old you is still in there. If you haven't strangled him."

Braxton burst into laughter. "I see you still got jokes, too."

"I try."

They both took breathers from the intensity of the quick descent into personal territory by downing several bites of food and commenting on the satisfactory taste.

"How'd you get into project management?"

Tiffany swallowed quickly. This conversation would be far more comfortable. "After I transferred from Pinkston, I changed my major to business and—"

"You were so gung-ho about teaching, though. What dissolved your passion?"

So much for a comfortable conversation. "Braxton, I'm not trying to take you on a guilt trip, here." She puckered her lips. "I do want to be honest with you, though."

"I wouldn't want it any other way."

After hesitating, Tiffany continued, "I guess I...I always saw myself getting married, having kids. White picket fence. My husband being the main breadwinner, my piddly teaching income paying for the luxuries—private school, vacations, spa treatments and shopping sprees from time to time. But when *that* happened between us, it was like the rose-colored-glasses came off my eyes. I realized that I couldn't depend on anyone else. If I was going to live a successful life, I needed a degree in a field where I could actually afford a decent standard of living all by myself."

Braxton gave a sharp whistle. "Tiff, that's deep. I'm sorry I caused you to give up on your passion."

"No"— she waved him off—"it was my decision. In hindsight, it was the best decision. I mean, even if I *do* get married someday, who's to say my husband won't ever get laid off or become ill. I won't be stuck out no matter what."

He grimaced playfully. "Please, you'll *never* be stuck out. Last I checked, you were a daddy's girl all the way. Spoiled rotten. Remember when he Western-Unioned you the money to buy those new Jordans the day they released? And then you and I drove to Houston and camped outside from like... midnight until the store opened at ten o'clock the next day? Froze our behinds off for those shoes!"

Tiffany smiled at the memory. Fighting back tears, she told Braxton, "My dad died. Four months ago."

Concern covered Braxton's face. He reached for Tiffany's hand across the table again.

She gladly responded, allowing him to comfort her with a slight squeeze.

"I'm so sorry. I remember how close you were to your father."

"Thanks." Tiffany squeezed back, thinking that would be the end of his touch. But he lingered, holding on for a few seconds longer than she'd expected. And she let him.

She dashed her mixed emotions—sadness and excitement—with a sip of water. "So what's up with you and your pops? As I recall it, you're supposed to be a preacher by now."

He didn't even try to cover with a chuckle this time. "My dad's still my dad. Reth Stoneworth. Running things at the church with the same fervor he used to run down the football field to make a touchdown."

"So, you gave up on preaching?"

"Yeah. Having a kid when you're not married kinda takes you out of the holy loop. Not that I was ever in it. People like my Dad...they're larger than life, you know? It's like, he's created this standard.

My other siblings are coming close. My oldest brother, Knox, is a veterinarian. The brother under me, Jarvis, is a civil engineer. My youngest brother, West, works with my dad at the church while he's attending seminary.

Our baby sister, Rainey, is killin' it at Arizona State, going straight through a six-year program to earn her Ph.D. in literature. She'll be Doctor Rainey Stoneworth next year."

"Wow," Tiffany marveled. "Your family is on it."

"Tell me about it." He clicked his cheek. "Hard to be a slacker around these overachievers."

"I wouldn't exactly call you a slacker, Braxton. You've got some things under your belt, too."

"Yeah, but it's taking more time than it should have. After I finished Pinkston, I played around for the first few years. Kept on drinking with the Lambdas. Got a job here and there, but nothing I could build a life on. Then I had a few wake-up calls and realized instead of fighting my father's influence, I needed to use it for all it was worth if I didn't want to end up living under a bridge somewhere or worse. And here I am, doing something that I enjoy, even though it's not quite what my Dad wanted for me."

"'Cause you're not preaching," Tiffany said.

"Right. But I'm thinking maybe he's given up on that. Might just be glad to have me working right now. Besides, it takes a certain kind of man to preach. I don't think I'm that man anymore. I mean, maybe I could lead a Bible study. But preach? No. Pastor? Heck no. Leave that to one of my other siblings."

With that sincere confession, Tiffany knew now that the real Braxton was still inside. A guy who didn't pretend to be on-top-of-the-world. A guy real enough to admit his shortcomings without trying to cover it up in red and gold. The guy she almost fell in love with.

A buzz emanated from Braxton's side of the table. He pulled his phone from his pocket. "Speaking of my father."

Tiffany busied herself eating more food while Braxton and his father conversed. She stared at her food, willing her tears to stay behind her eyelids. Just listening to someone else talk to their father was excruciating.

To her dismay, her tears fell across the rim of her

eyes. She had to swipe them away.

"Um, Dad, let me call you back. All right?" Braxton put down his phone. "Tiff, what's wrong?"

"You…talking to your dad," her voice creaked. She swiped again. "I'd give anything to hear my dad's voice again."

After a long silence, Braxton said, "Hold on to the hope you have in Christ. You'll see him again."

"So true" she agreed, thankful that Braxton had brought the comfort of God's word to mind. "It's hard to move forward in the meantime."

"I'm sure your father would be very proud of you. Everything you've accomplished. You've got your own business. Runnin' thangs," he drawled.

Laughter trickled through Tiffany's lips. "He was glad. He knew about the business. He still hounded me for giving up teaching. Just like you."

"So you never told him why you changed majors?"

"No. And you'd better be glad I didn't. My daddy would have kicked your behind."

Braxton puffed out his chest. "I don't blame him. The first dude who breaks my baby's heart is gonna be chased down in the streets like he took five dollars from the offering basket."

"Well"—Tiffany dried her eyes completely— "they say everybody plays the fool once."

"Except this time, you weren't the fool. *I* was. And I'm sorry."

She let the apology sink in. "Thank you. And I'm

sorry I didn't give you a chance to rectify the situation."

He raised an eyebrow. "Truth be told, Tiff, with the frame of mind I was in, I probably wouldn't have rectified it. I would have *wrecked* it. I really did lose my mind when I first pledged. That's why it took me another year to graduate. It was probably best that you left when you did."

She nodded.

"But I think it's best that we're meeting again now," he continued. "Even if we are competing for the same contract."

"Yes, we are. And I really don't want to discuss business tonight."

"Right. Don't want you tryna to steal my winning ideas."

"As if." Tiffany tried to snarl, but the mean glance melted under the heat of Braxton's gorgeous smile.

Chapter 9

The next morning, Tiffany checked in with the middle school secretary and found their break room several minutes before the bell rang. Unlike the elementary teachers' lounge, this one didn't double as a workroom. There were tables and chairs along with a television. Deja and Braxton were watching CNN when Tiffany entered the room.

The sight of him and the new memories created only the previous evening combined to send a much-needed blast of energy through her veins. After leaving the restaurant, Tiffany had showered and dressed down into her footed one-piece pajamas. She'd downed another energy drink to make it through the emails and attachments related to her open projects, and logged in work hours before heading to bed.

Sleep eluded her, despite a tiring four hours worth of work. The energy drink still hadn't worn off. She considered taking Nyquil to bring her down, but wasn't sure of how the two concoctions might interact. The last thing she needed was to wind up dead in the middle of trying to land this contract.

Not to mention she'd also miss out on this *thing*—whatever it was—with Braxton.

"Morning," she said, trying to sound as professional as she had the day before. If Deja sniffed chemistry between her competitors, she'd definitely use it to her advantage.

"Hey," from Deja, whose eyes were glued to the set.

"Hello," from Braxton. He stood and shook her hand.

Good, he's playing it cool.

The three compared schedules. She and Braxton had the first class together. All three had chapel at nine-thirty, a weekly requirement for all students and staff.

"I'll see you in the sanctuary," Deja said to Braxton.

"I hope you see *God* in the sanctuary," he directed.

Tiffany hid behind his shoulder so Deja wouldn't see her laughing.

Deja didn't reply. Really, how could she? She flew out of that lounge.

"Braxton, why'd you do her like that?" Tiff pretended to fuss.

"I'm a gentleman, so I won't repeat what was offered before you walked in," he said with a straight face.

Classic Deja. "My name is Paul, and that's between y'all."

Tiffany and Braxton weren't ready for what they saw in Miss Capshaw's class. From studies in the two education classes she took as a sophomore and her own memories of junior high, Tiffany knew that middle school kids were rough. But never this rough. The kids were up out of their seats doing everything from sharpening pencils to popping bra straps. The few on the front row who were trying to listen to the teacher couldn't because of the ruckus. Every few seconds, Miss Capshaw had to address someone who was off task, which led to a stand-off, seeing as no twelve-year-old wants to be shamed in front of their classmates.

The teacher slapped the paper she was reading from against her thigh. "Nathaniel, put your feet flat on the floor!"

"I'm just trying to tie my shoe!" he retorted.

He could have just as easily bent over and tied his shoe like a normal person, but no. Nathaniel had propped his Nike up on his desktop.

The girl in front of him, who had long black hair, turned around. "Don't be putting your nasty shoe on my hair!"

"Girl, I ain't messin' with your hair! But I will if you want me to." He reached for her long mane.

She screamed and threw a pink eraser at him.

"That's enough!" Miss Capshaw yelled. "You two want to go to the office?"

"He started it! And you can't send me to the office because I didn't want a boy's feet on my hair!"

On and on, the "lesson" continued with a series of interruptions.

Tiffany couldn't even remember what the kids were supposed to be learning, which she noted in her documentation.

Braxton, who was sitting in one of the back desks next to her, looked up from his laptop, leaned in and whispered, "These kids are about to make me go Incredible Hulk on them."

"Remain objective," Tiffany prompted him. "Record what you see without judgment." *Why am I giving him hints on how to beat me out of this contract?*

He flexed his arms in Hulk-fashion.

Tiffany giggled.

The little girl sitting in front of them, who had been quiet for the most part, turned around. Her wrists layered in bracelets, she smiled shyly at Tiffany and said, "This class is bad, right?"

"Janeria! Turn around! Leave our guests alone!" came from Miss Capshaw.

Quickly, the girl complied. But, of course, that made everyone else in the room focus on Tiffany and Braxton.

"Hi!" Shoe-tying boy hollered clear from the other side of the class. His word prompted almost everyone else to give greetings as well.

For once, the students were giving their attention to an adult.

Tiffany nodded silently.

Braxton growled, "Don't 'hi' me. Not after the disrespectful way you've been treating your teacher."

A few kids bowed their heads, faced the front again.

With a twirl of his finger, Braxton instructed them all to give Miss Capshaw their attention.

Tiffany sat amazed at how just a few words from Braxton had more weight than a hundred from their teacher. It was as though 'Daddy' had come home for work. All of a sudden, there was increased order as the threat of swift, no-excuses-offered-or-accepted discipline loomed in the atmosphere.

The teacher passed a thankful glance toward Braxton. "Now, class, as I was saying. You probably remember from your social studies classes in elementary school that women didn't have the right to vote. To this day, people are still arguing over who should and shouldn't be allowed to vote in our country. So let me know if you agree with this statement: Every adult in the United States should have the right to vote."

Hands flew in the air. Miss Capshaw called on a boy on the front row. "No."

The class roared with reaction. "What?" from some and "That's right" from others.

In a matter of seconds, the room was filled with chatter again, though at least this time they were talking about the subject. Tiffany wrote: *This was an interesting topic, yet the students were unable to benefit from the academic discussion due to an inability to hear one another's thoughts.*

Suddenly, an idea for an activity she'd learned in

one of her undergrad classes (before she switched her major) entered Tiffany's thoughts. As the students continued debating—or better yet, arguing—between the teacher's empty threats, Tiffany got the woman's attention.

Frustration written on her young face, she approached Tiffany. "I'm so sorry. This is one of my most rambunctious classes. They're wound up and it's not even nine o'clock yet!"

"No worries. I've got an idea that might help."

"Please! Anything is better than this." Miss Capshaw stepped back.

Tiffany then realized that the teacher had moved out of the way to give Tiffany the floor. Not exactly what she'd been expecting to do, but she might as well because Miss Capshaw was right—it really couldn't get worse.

At the front of the classroom, Tiffany briefed Miss Capshaw on the plan.

"Okay, listen up, everyone, our guest, Miss Warren, would like to try an activity with us."

About half the class stopped talking.

Braxton cleared his throat.

The rest obeyed his unspoken demand.

"Here's what we're going to do," Tiffany explained as adrenaline pumped through her system. *I'm actually teaching a class of kids right now.* "Miss Capshaw has several statements. When she reads a statement, you're going to literally take a stand on the issue. If you strongly agree, you'll stand all the way to my right." Tiffany motioned to the area nearest the pencil sharpener. "If you strongly disagree, you'll stand all the way to my left. If you're a 'maybe', you'll stand here at the Smartboard, where I'm standing now. If you're somewhere in between the middle but leaning toward one side or the other, stand at a place that corresponds with how you feel about the issue. Got it?"

"Yes, ma'am," they chorused.

"Okay. Miss Capshaw, hit it."

Energetically, the teacher read, "Women should be treated the same as men."

The students raced to their spots, apparently excited to be out of their seats and engaged in the lesson. Most of the kids crowded around the "agree" side, though there were several who disagreed strongly. A small group was standing in the middle.

"Now," Tiffany continued instruction, "Take a minute to talk with those around you. Make sure you absolutely agree with everyone who's standing with you. If your opinion isn't as strong as those around you, or if you're somehow off from those around you, you might need to take a step a little closer to the middle. You have two minutes. Mr. Stoneworth, can you time us?"

"*Stone*-worth?" one of the boys teased, which brought about giggles and laughter.

"Yeah. You might know my dad, Reth Stoneworth. He played in the NFL."

"Oh, for reals?" the teaser said. "I wanna play

football, too."

Somehow, the letters N-F-L had ended the snickers and added another layer of respect with the boys.

"Timer's ready," Braxton said, cell phone in hand.

"Okay." Tiffany reminded the students of their task, then set them off. After two minutes, she told the students they needed to move if their stance had somehow changed through the conversation with peers. Four students moved, which gave her an opportunity to ask them why they'd changed opinions as other listened intently for the rationale. Then she asked the extremists to share their opinion and why. On the cuff and in a zone of sorts, Tiffany asked probing questions to challenge students' reasoning: Should men still hold doors open for women? What about domestic violence—should women be prosecuted the same as men despite physical differences? Does it matter how people treat you— can't you still accomplish anything regardless of other people's views or actions?

Miss Capshaw jumped in with a few questions of her own.

In the midst of the more structured debate, the bell rang.

"Awwww man!" several kids lamented. "Can we finish tomorrow?"

"Yes, we can," Miss Capshaw promised.

The kids cheered as they grabbed their belongings and left the room. Tiffany smiled as they passed her.

"Thanks, Miss Warren. You'd make a great teacher."

An inner sunshine warmed Tiffany's heart. "Thank you."

Braxton joined the women at the board. "I was thinking the same thing."

Miss Capshaw tilted her head and asked Tiffany, "You sure you didn't miss your calling?"

The question was more poignant than the teacher probably realized.

"I think I'm good for now," Tiffany answered. The fact that she was positioned in the middle, where the undecided people stood during the activity, didn't escape her.

"Thank you both for your help. I'll use that strategy as often as possible," Miss Capshaw spewed with excitement. "I know you're here for the project and all, but if you've got any more ideas, please come back and share them with me. My planning period is from 2:00 – 3:15."

"If I think of any more, I sure will," Tiffany said. "Thanks for having us." She picked up her purse and materials. Already, she was thinking of a few more methods that would work well with an active class full of pre-teens.

As they exited the classroom, Braxton eyed Tiffany up and down.

"What?"

"I see you. Miss *Warren. Teacher extraordinaire.* You've got all kinds of tricks up your sleeves, huh?"

"No. I just…I know stuff."

"I see."

After Tiffany made a stop at the restroom, they traveled on to the chapel, which was held in the middle school's cafetorium. Coming in a few minutes late meant they'd be seated toward the rear again. Those chapel ushers weren't playing – every class, every adult was seated on their little row as they entered. No going to the back when closer seats were vacant.

Deja must have gotten there earlier. She was seated toward the middle.

"We need *these* ushers at my dad's church," Braxton joked.

"Right."

Seated on stage were Mr. McDonald, Rhonda, and a few other people Tiffany recognized from walking around the building. After an opening prayer, Rhonda took the microphone and sang *Indescribable* solo.

You put the starts in the sky and you know them by name.

Tiffany closed her eyes and swayed to the simple melody as she contemplated the depths and heights of God's majesty. As Rhonda continued giving praise, Tiffany formed mental images. She envisioned lightning bolts coming and asking God, "Where do you want us to go next?" She'd read the scripture the lyricist had drawn from in the book of Job, when God finally put an end to the speculations of a pained man and his friends. *The nerve of us trying to put God's thoughts into the little boxes in our heads.*

Braxton hummed along softly as well. Actually, he was doing a little more than humming. He took it to another level, throwing in a little falsetto and some ad-libbing that could have been included in a professional recording.

Following the song, a young man from a sister school stepped to the stage to deliver a message from Hebrews 11:6, using the King James version of the Bible. He focused on the last part of the scripture, "…he is a rewarder of them that diligently seek him," encouraging the students to recognize that God rewards those who seek His face. "I don't know what your Christmas list looks like, but I can tell you this: if you find God, you'll find the other things, too."

The adults in the room nodded, kids watched silently.

Tiffany wondered if this was part of the reason she was suffering financially. It had to be. She certainly hadn't been spending as much time with the Lord as she used to—not with starting the business and working seemingly twenty-five hours a day to stay on top of deadlines. *No wonder I'm near bankrupt.*

Still, she was asking God for *more* work, which would probably require subcontracting, which would mean someone else to keep tabs on.

Braxton elbowed her. "Let me show you something." He opened his phone and scrolled. Tapped. Then he handed it to Tiffany.

She read Genesis 15:1. *After these things the word of the Lord came unto Abram in a vision, saying, Fear not, Abram: I am thy shield, and thy exceeding great reward.*

She looked up at him, somewhat puzzled.

He whispered, "God *is* the reward. Not the things."

She read again. *I am thy shield, and thy exceeding great reward.* The Truth of the last phrase hit her: God's plan doesn't revolve around stuff. It revolved around Him. "That's deep, Braxton."

Braxton winked at her. "Gotta know the Word."

But the revelation kind of kicked Tiffany in the gut. She wanted stuff. Things. Much more than she or her parents had ever experienced. Granted, God was no small reward...but what about the *stuff*?

Being in the scant back section had it's rewards, too. Tiffany could ask without disruption, "What about John 10:10? Jesus came for us to have an abundant life?"

Braxton nearly snatched the phone from her again. He navigated again, passed it back to her.

This time, she read John 14:6. *Jesus saith unto him, I am the way, the truth, and the life: no man cometh unto the Father, but by me.*

Braxton spoke quietly, "Once again, it's not the things. His life in us *is* the abundant life."

With Braxton's explanation, Tiffany could only sit and ponder her goals and aspirations. She had founded her own company to relieve stress and try her hand at something new. Theoretically. But this train of thought wasn't headed toward theory. It stopped at her true motivations. Was she in it to manage projects or control her own destiny? Had she taken this leap in faith or had she made a mad dash to be her own boss in the throes of frustration?

Going further back, she tried to remember if she'd even talked to God before leaving Pinkston and changing her major.

No. I didn't. She'd been too hurt to talk to God. *Too hurt to talk to God?*

Those words reverberated in her spirit. She'd been too hurt to talk to God since her father died, too.

Tiffany didn't know what else the preacher had said. The Holy Spirit had taken over the sermon and, in the end, pulled at her to fully return to Him.

A closing prayer by Mr. McDonald sent everyone back to their classrooms.

Tiffany and Braxton were going separate ways for the rest of the day. He gave her a tiny wave.

"Wait. Do you always create your own side commentary for the sermon?"

"Not always," he said. "Only when I hear something that needs some clarification in the Word. Why?"

"God used you to open my eyes today. More than you know. I think *you're* the one who might be missing your calling."

"You been talking to my Father?" he joked.

"Depends on which father you're referring to."

"Touche."

Chapter 10

Amongst a horde of middle school students flowing toward the parking lot, Tiffany spotted Braxton only seconds after school dismissed. She stepped off the cement pathway onto the grass to allow the stream of kids to pass as she waited for her comrade.

"How'd it go?" she asked.

"Fine. Went to a religion class. They had a roundtable, included me in the discussion. Had to clear up a few misconceptions."

"Wish I could have been there."

"How'd it go with you?"

"Pretty good," Tiffany replied. "One thing for sure about middle school is that there's no such thing as a dull day."

"Hey!" Braxton pointed to their left. "There's the agricultural building. We're supposed to check it out some time. You wanna do it now?"

Fear gripped Tiffany's chest. Visions of an animal charging toward her reappeared. "No. Might have to skip out on that one."

"I don't know, Tiff. I think they're pretty proud of that program. I mean, if you don't want the contract that's no problem for me." He tugged at his pin-striped lapel. "I'm just sayin'."

She knew he was right...but animals. They were

unpredictable. Wild. *Animals*. Not to be trusted. The only other available time would be Wednesday. She'd have to work up her nerves before tomorrow if she planned on including notes about this portion in her report.

"I'll do it another time."

"Cool."

Her phone vibrated in her pocket once. Twice. She kept in stride with Braxton as she answered, "Hey, Momma."

"Tiff, did you pay the yard man?"

"Yeah—wait—no. I was going to handle it Friday." Tiffany pretended she was unsure, but in truth she couldn't afford to pay the gardener in full before the first of the month. Her main client was taking the entire thirty days to pay her most recent invoice. And she couldn't say one word until they were past due.

"Well, he ain't come in almost a month and I just got a notice from the city! Said if I don't cut the grass in five days, they'll cut it and send me a bill for seventy-five dollars!" she fussed.

Tiffany stopped. Thinking. "Can you call Uncle Sammy?"

"You know I don't want Sammy sniffin' around here, tryin' to see what else of your father's he can take," she fussed. "Oooh, I miss your daddy so much. Even though your father didn't actually cut the grass himself, he made sure it got done and inspected it, too. It's the little things, you know?"

"I know, Momma. I'm sorry. I should have taken care of this sooner." This wouldn't have happened if she'd had some duckies in the bank. *I gotta stay on my grind.*

Braxton, who had stopped with her, was staring at the children boarding busses, but the worry etched in his forehead told Tiffany that he was listening to her conversation.

"I'll call you back in a few minutes. Bye."

She disconnected the call and continued walking, contemplating her next move. Daddy had always been Momma's rock. Tiffany didn't want to let her mother down on this thing…she might not make it back up again.

"Sounds serious," Braxton commented.

"Wait!" She stopped again. "You got a lawnmower?"

"Yeah."

"You know how to cut grass?"

"Does Patti Labelle make sweet potato pies?"

Tiffany squeezed her eyes shut, trying to remain focused in the presence of his hilarity. "Okay, Braxton, this is a lot to ask. But is there any way you could go to my mom's house today and cut the grass? I'll pay you Friday."

He shrugged. "Gladly. Pro bono."

"No, I don't want you to—"

"I *want* to." Braxton's eyes leapt upon hers.

All she could say was, "Okay."

"You want to follow me to my house? We can put

the lawnmower in the back of my truck and ride to your mom's together."

"Okay. I'll give you gas money."

"Tiff. Stop. I don't need you to give me anything," Braxton nearly scolded. "I got this."

A sense or relief, or security, or both swept over Tiffany. She quelled the urge to wrap her arms around Braxton's neck and give him the biggest hug. *Keep calm.* "Perfect."

"Let's exchange numbers in case we get separated on the highway," Braxton suggested.

She complied and saved him to her contacts.

They drove to a quaint neighborhood with the kinds of homes realtors often recommended for first-time homebuyers: small, low-maintenance, in an older neighborhood. His home fit the bill exactly. Not what she'd imagined for the son of a man who was probably quite well off. With this revelation, she was quite proud of Braxton. He was roughing it on his own. The Lexus, which he parked in the garage, was most likely more of an investment than a splurge. Tiffany knew from experience that potential clients were impressed by nice rides.

Maybe one day, she'd have her own Lexus.

Or maybe not. If she could land clients like Mr. McDonald, who seemed more interested in heart than appearance, she could roll in a Honda forever.

Braxton hoisted the lawnmower over the tailgate

as Tiffany looked on. Hopefully, she was admiring the muscles that were visible in the t-shirt he'd changed into for the task ahead. Those reps at the gym came in handy with the chicks.

Tiff was no ordinary chick. In fact, she wasn't in the "chick" category at all. She wasn't someone he hoped to conquer with the quickness first and see where things went afterward. Actually, he hadn't done that to or with anyone for a while now. He used to enjoy that lifestyle: a new woman every few weeks, sometimes juggling more than one at a time, watching his frat brothers' reactions when he walked into the party with a different piece of eye-candy on his arm.

But that was getting old. And every time he got a picture of Brianna in his phone and saw her morphing from a chubby, long-lashed infant into a beautiful child on her way to becoming a young lady, he envisioned his baby girl getting played the way he played somebody else's baby girl.

Yeah. It was getting old.

He slammed the gate shut and opened the passenger's door for Tiffany. "Watch your step." Braxton secured her elbow as she climbed into the truck, then hopped into his side. "Where to?" He'd assumed Tiffany's mother still lived east of Dallas, which wasn't terribly far. But it really didn't matter where the woman lived, he'd drive anywhere with Tiffany.

The close confines of the truck caused her

perfume and the remnants of his cologne to mix, creating a soft scent all their own. The few feet between them was unmistakably charged as both gratitude and attraction mingled with Tiffany thanking him once again and his flirty wink in response.

"Take twenty east."

"Roger."

They taunted each other briefly about Red Sea Academy, going back and forth about which one of them would win.

"Don't sleep on Deja," Tiffany warned. "She's got a decent company behind her."

"I can't, with her."

Tiffany laughed. "Yeah, let's stop talking about her. I don't want to be up all night repenting." She opened her purse and pulled out something red.

With his eyes on the road, Braxton couldn't quite make it out. "What's that?"

"An energy drink. Gotta keep myself going, you know?"

"Does it work?"

"Yeah."

"Is it good for you?"

She chuckled as she twisted off the top. "Probably not."

He put a hand over hers. "Wait. Put it down for now."

"What? Why?"

"Because." He tried to think of how to explain

what he heard coming from within him. Telling a woman to slow down these days was akin to revoking her independent-woman card and sending her to slave over a hot stove. "Maybe you don't need it."

"Braxton, I know my own body. I know my workload. I need this drink."

Those four words—*I need this drink*—confirmed his unction. "You drink them every day?"

"Yep." She slid her hands away, finished opening the cap, and raised the tiny can to her lips.

"Wait. What if you try today without it. Then you'll be able to see if your body has adjusted and is able to handle life without a sip."

She screwed the lid back on and tossed the container back in her purse. "Braxton, why are you policing me?"

He'd have to come clean. "Because I know what it's like to depend on a substance to make it through the day."

Silence. He studied the road ahead.

"Sooo…what happened?"

"Psssh, what *didn't* happen is probably a better question." He draped his arm over the steering wheel, easing into a casual tone. He hoped Tiffany wouldn't overreact. "All the partying, the drinking…catches up with you after a while. At first, I was only drinking on the weekends. Then a little Hennessey after work. Before I knew it, I was drinking every day. Then twice a day. Fooled around and got a D-U-I. License suspended for nine months. Went to a rehab. God did an intervention on me. I'm grateful I made it through—not everyone lives to tell the story."

"Wow."

He clicked his cheek. "But don't worry. I got my license back. And insurance."

"Uh, you'd better, seeing as you're driving *me* around this very moment."

Yep, God is good. Braxton repeated to himself for the millionth time since his ordeal. Too many innocent people had lost their lives to irresponsible drinkers.

"This is going to sound like a silly question, but what was jail like?"

"Man. It was a jungle in there. Every man for himself. My sense of humor came in quite handy when dudes tried to size me up. By the second day, they were calling me the tall Kevin Hart."

"How many days were you behind bars?"

"I got arrested on a Saturday, so I was incarcerated until Monday morning. My dad got me out. Told me it was the first and last time he'd get me out of jail. Then he gave me an award-winning son-don't-ever-let-me-down-again speech. But I deserved it. And I needed it. At the time, getting arrested seemed like the worst event of my entire life. But now I realize what a blessing it was to be taken off the streets before I could hurt anyone, least of all myself. I know unequivocally that I don't deserve my next breath. Every second is another unmerited gift. I thank God for saving me from myself. He showed me who He is: The Great I *Am*."

"What a testimony," Tiffany gasped.

"It's all about Him."

"Which is exactly why you should share it with people. I mean, maybe not with *everybody*, but people need hope."

"You think people want someone with a DUI preaching to them about what they should and shouldn't do?" Braxton asked.

"You don't have to tell people what to do. Just tell them what *God* did in your life. I think He will take it from there. If more of us shared our mess-ups and His fix-ups, people wouldn't feel so condemned about being human."

"I don't think I'm ready to tell the world all my business. Not sure if my dad would appreciate me dragging our family name through the mud, especially not after all he paid to keep the situation under wraps in an instant-information society."

Braxton switched lanes and contemplated speeding past an eighteen-wheeler but decided to be patient instead. Any traffic violation would mean another meeting with the attorney to prevent his case from possible review in light of another infraction.

Braxton was thankful that Tiffany didn't seem spooked by his DUI confession. Somehow, people seemed to give him a break because just about everyone knew what it was like to have one too many.

Does Tiffany drink?

It seemed improbable that she hadn't taken a swig or two in her day. Then again, it was also highly unlikely that a woman in their age bracket hadn't slept with anyone yet.

"So," Tiffany chirped, "I have a deep, dark secret of my own."

"Okaaay." *Oh, God, no. Really, God, I'm talking to You – No!* Braxton refused to let himself consider all the possible options she might throw at him. Tiffany's a fugitive? A shoplifter? An ex-stripper?

"You ready?"

"Go. I can handle it."

"Just before you pledged, I had a crush on you."

Braxton grinned. "That was a pleasant surprise."

"People kept saying we were together since they saw us together all the time. And the more they said it, I got this picture in my mind. Of us. Crazy, huh?"

"How's it crazy?"

"Because," she sang, "we were friends. A man and a woman can be friends, you know?"

"True." He supposed.

"Anyway, I thought that was kinda funny."

Braxton searched his mental women-thesaurus. Did "funny" mean interesting? Good? Bad? Was this an invitation?

When he couldn't pinpoint the motive, he decided the best thing to do was ask. If they were destined to remain friends only, there was no need in playing games. "Why are you telling me now?"

"It just came to mind."

"I feel like I should rip a piece of paper out of my spiral and draw three boxes on it, then you can check like, don't like, or maybe."

She gave him the side-eye. "We're not in kindergarten."

"What kind of kindergarten were you in? I couldn't spell 'maybe' until fourth quarter of the first grade, two-minute warning. You musta been with the smart kids."

Tiffany doubled over, cackling. "I was in a regular kindergarten!"

"Naw. You had some advanced-ness in your group."

Her hair bounced back in place as she brought herself to an upright position again. "Whoo!" she howled. "Oh my gosh, you almost made me miss the exit. Get off here."

She guided him the rest of the route. They arrived at a modest one-story home surrounded by a whole lotta grass that definitely needed a trim. Otherwise, the brick house seemed as well-kept as the other dwellings in the cul-de-sac.

He parked the truck and cut off the engine.

When he reached to unsnap his seatbelt, Tiffany seized his hand. "Thank you, Braxton. Coming back to this house is tough, since my dad's not here. You've made me laugh on this trip. I haven't been able to do that since my dad got sick, almost a year ago."

"My pleasure."

Chapter 11

It was a good thing Braxton had worn a rugged pair of jeans and reapplied his deodorant. After meeting Mrs. Warren and one of Tiffany's sisters, their momma put Braxton to work!

After he finished cutting the yard, Mrs. Warren asked Braxton to get up on a chair and change the time on a clock that was still running on daylight savings time, although it had ended the previous week.

After fixing the clock, he tightened a pipe under the kitchen sink, fixed a door handle, and beat nails into a few slats in the back fence until they fell back into place.

He took a quick break when Mrs. Warren brought out a glass of iced tea. Braxton dropped the hammer on the grass. Carefully, he let the nails he'd been dangling from his mouth fall into his right left hand while he took the glass from Tiffany's mother.

"Thank you, ma'am." He sipped the refreshing drink.

She inspected his work. "You doin' a mighty fine job."

Mrs. Warren looked toward the back door, then quickly at him again. "Since my husband ain't here, I gotta give you the shakedown."

He swallowed hard and ducked his head low to

make sure he was hearing correctly. "The shakedown, ma'am?"

"Listen here. My daughter's proud. She's independent. But don't let that fool you. She's also sweet and kind and loyal to a fault. But she's stubborn."

Had he not already known these things for himself, he might have been confused.

"My point is, she's trying really hard right now to hold it together, but she's a human being. This business she started, it's been a rough go. She's wearin' herself out. But I believe she's gonna be fine. Don't you go gettin' her all distracted. Her daddy might be gone, but Momma Bear is still here. You understand?"

"Yes, ma'am. I do."

She snatched the unfinished glass from him.

"But I—"

"That's enough to carry you through."

Mrs. Warren yanked up a fist full of her long skirt's fabric and moseyed on back to the house.

Braxton wasn't quite sure what had transpired. He'd been interrogated by fathers, uncles, and big brothers, but never a mother.

As he beat the final nails in place, he realized that Mrs. Warren's threat was somehow scarier that the ones he'd received before. When a man says he's gonna get you, that means he's gonna come straight at you and pound your face. But when a woman has revenge on her mind, she's not going to square up.

There was no telling when or where she might attack. An angry woman could suddenly appear from behind a light pole on a dark street corner and go straight crazy on you. She could go after your car, your legs, your new girlfriend. Getting the "shakedown" from a woman was definitely more frightening.

Does her mother know Jesus?

Finally done with the fence, Braxton entered the small but tidy kitchen. He wiped sweat from his forehead and above his lip. "Anything else, Mrs. Warren?"

"Yes, Braxton," Tiffany answered for her mother. "Here. Have something to eat."

Tiffany, her sister Tina and their mother had been tooling around in the kitchen the whole time Braxton was working.

Braxton didn't mind being put to work. Despite the fact that his father played in the NFL and could afford to hire plenty of help, Reth Stoneworth insisted that his sons learn how to handle simple handiwork around the house and perform routine tasks on a car—flat tires, oil changes and such.

"Every man ought to be able to complete small jobs with his own hands. You don't want to have to wait and depend on people for everything."

Those lessons had benefitted Braxton greatly today.

Braxton took a bite of the hearty sandwich Tiffany gave him. Sitting there at the table with three women smiling as he chewed, he suddenly got the feeling that maybe he had something on his chin.

He swallowed. "Is everything okay?"

Mrs. Warren gave a sweet smile. "I was just telling Tiffany I really like you. I hope she don't do anything to run you off like she did the last one."

He coughed. "The last one?"

Tiffany protested, "Momma, quit."

"She's not lying," her sister said. She turned to Braxton. "Tiffany is a good person. But she doesn't tolerate foolishness. At all."

"Why should she?" Braxton asked.

Tiffany crossed her arms. "Thank you. And for the record, that guy was *not* a potential interest. He was a co-worker. I was working a project on this side of town, and we only met here after-hours because Starbucks was too crowded and noisy."

Mrs. Warren gave Tiffany duck-lips. "Mmmm hmmm."

"We'd better get going now. Braxton and I have one more day of observations at Red Sea Academy."

"Oh. Are you two working together?" Tina asked.

"No. We're competing," Tiffany informed them.

"So only one of you will get the job?" from her mother.

"Yep," Braxton confirmed. "We've got one more competitor, but Tiffany and I are pretty sure the prize will go to one of us."

Tina's eyes widened. "So what happens to the loser?"

"Loser goes home," Braxton said.

He'd hoped to see a snarky, bratty face on Tiffany, but instead he saw anxiety. Fear, perhaps.

Braxton downed the ham sandwich and chips as the women talked about their Thanksgiving plans with extended family; who was bringing the turkey, the greens, the sweet potato pie. He noticed that Tiffany didn't have much to say about the dinner.

As soon as he took the last bite, Tiffany stood. "Gotta go." She slid Braxton's plate from him and transported it to the sink.

Braxton and the rest rose as well.

Mrs. Warren gave him a hug and thanked him for everything he'd done around the house.

Tina gave him a side-hug. "'Preciate you, bro."

"No problem."

Braxton went outside to load the lawnmower back in the truck, leaving Tiffany inside to say good-byes to her family and whatever else they needed to say while he wasn't around.

When she joined him at the truck, she was wearing a goofy smile.

"Something funny?"

"My mom."

He helped her into the truck. "What happened?"

"She wants to adopt you."

"I don't know. Somehow I get the feeling your mom would have me working day and night around this joint." Braxton chortled, walking back to his side of the vehicle. He stepped into his spot and secured himself. He started the truck.

She nudged his arm with hers on the armrest. "Thanks for being a good sport."

He stopped, not wanting to spoil the moment with driving. "It's the least I could do after what happened to us."

Tiffany exhaled. Turned her body to face him. "Can we forget about all that? Just start over?"

"Couldn't have said it better myself."

The close quarters of the truck suddenly became even smaller as he leaned toward Tiffany. Her hair fell onto his cheek. Finally, he was doing what he'd dreamed of doing all those years ago.

Braxton leaned over and captured her lips with his. Once. Twice.

She pulled away.

Braxton opened his eyes, wondering why on earth Tiffany had ended their kiss. But when he witnessed her thirty-two teeth sparkling at him and noted the quickness of her breath, the answer was clear. She'd felt the sharp thrills flooding through her body, too.

"Whew," Tiffany said, "it's a good thing we *didn't* do that when I was nineteen."

Braxton returned her smile. He wiped the slickness from her bottom lip with his fingertip. "Here's to a new beginning."

"Cheers," she seconded.

In the absence of glasses, they gave each other dap.

To keep from spoiling the moment, Braxton turned on some gospel jazz.

Tiffany unzipped her denim jacket, took it off, and draped it across her chest. She snuggled up to her door, hiding her hands under the makeshift blanket. Before he even made it to the highway, she was asleep. Ten minutes later, she was snoring. Another five and there was a slight drool coming from the left corner of her mouth.

If he hadn't felt sorry for her, he might have taken a picture. But she'd been telling the truth about her energy level, and Mrs. Warren had been forthright about her daughter's dedication to work.

Tiffany was tired. Working-on-the-railroad-track-in-1905 tired.

He heard her phone ring and instinctively grabbed it from her jacket pocket and silenced the ringer with a quick tap to the side of the phone before she could wake.

Whoever and whatever it was would have to wait until Tiffany got her much-needed rest.

Braxton took a longer route home. The soft rattle of her breathing made him smile as he thought of what it would be like for her to sleep this close to him every night. Forever.

The vision scared him, actually. *What am I thinking?* He couldn't jump into a relationship now. He was still building his life after the DUI. Still needed to get things straight with his daughter. Still wanted to prove to his father that he wasn't a big mess-up. Red Sea Academy should be his focus because it was the ticket to his future.

And the only thing standing in the way of his big comeback was the woman he didn't want to lose again.

He tried to think through a good ending to this dilemma. If he won, he'd be set for the next year and add a distinguished client to his list. Jeff McDonald was well-known in the community. The Red Sea really would be the Red Sea—it would pave a way to the promised land.

But Tiffany. She'd be struggling, trying to take care of herself and her mother.

If she won, Braxton honestly didn't know how he'd handle it. She might need his help. She might even ask him to subcontract. *Could I work for Tiff?*

Probably not. There was no way he could work for her with so much chemistry between them. It would be a disaster.

Beyond that, his competitive side never jived with the adage "if you can't beat 'em, join 'em." Braxton knew he was one hundred percent wrong, but he wasn't sure if his ego could take Tiffany winning. That would be like letting a girl dunk on him in basketball.

He sighed and resigned to do whatever it took to win the contract and save their budding relationship. It was best for both of them.

Chapter 12

Listening to Braxton had cost Tiffany dearly. Without the energy drink, she'd fallen asleep on the way back from her mother's house, and she hadn't been able to pull herself together once she got home. She crashed in bed at 9:30 and slept through the morning. Even with seven and a half hours of sleep, she still needed something to get her going.

Am I addicted to that stuff?

She settled on a cup of coffee from Grandy's Restaurant on her way to Red Sea Academy. The stop meant she was running later than normal and ended up in the drop-off line with parents. She had no time to fraternize with Braxton or Deja after getting her last itinerary from Rhonda.

The caffeine quick-started Tiffany's nerves and pepped her for a day in high school. As she walked through the halls with students closer to her height, Tiffany felt at ease. These were people she could relate to easily. These students were old enough to have been her little sisters and brothers instead of her nieces, nephews or even her own kids.

And the class couldn't have been more interesting: forensic science. The teacher had yellow crime tape streaming around the room with outlines of bodies taped along the walls. *How cool is this?* Tiffany got busy noting the extra touches in the room.

The teacher, Mr. Vorhees, didn't do much teaching after the bell rang. The students were seated in groups of four. He asked one person from each team to give an account of the group's case status. Then he set them free to continue with their projects, which Tiffany gathered was to determine the cause of death for a victim. With the teacher's permission, Tiffany circled the room and observed students' research using virtual simulators, notes and PG-rated photos from the "crime scene", and medical databases. The kids were engrossed in complicated discussions and mini-debates, theorizing and proving or disproving one another with facts.

Mr. Vorhees rotated to each group, asking questions and guiding students without assuming the lead.

To say the least, Tiffany was impressed. She wished she'd been in a class like this. *These kids have it made.*

Five minutes before the bell rang, Mr. Vorhees instructed the students to find a stopping point and journal their findings for the day so they could pick up where they'd start the next day.

Tiffany slipped out of Mr. Vorhees's room and crossed to the main hallway for a Spanish class. Again, she introduced herself to the teacher, Mrs. Treet, and tried to take an inconspicuous spot. Before the class was called to order, she got a text.

BRAXTON: Good Morning. How's it going?

TIFFANY: Back atcha. It's all good. You visit the forensic science class? AMAZING!
BRAXTON: No. Art. Now I'm in Physics.
TIFFANY: Ouch! Sorry.
BRAXTON: Enjoyed yesterday.
TIFFANY: Ditto.
BRAXTON: Stop tryna act like old boy in Ghost.

She stopped to laugh.

TIFFANY: Thanks again for helping my mom.
BRAXTON: Any time.
TIFFANY: Kiss wasn't so bad either.
BRAXTON: Ditto.

She gasped, "No he didn't!"

"Perdoname," the teacher spoke.

Tiffany looped up from her screen to find thirty sets of eyes focused on her. She must have missed the bell.

Someone whispered to Tiffany, "She said pardon me."

"Oh, I'm so sorry. I didn't realize we'd begun," Tiffany apologized to everyone.

The teacher gave a disapproving glance. "Si. La clase empezo."

My bad.

Tiffany turned off her phone and got back to work, though she had no idea what to write seeing as she didn't understand Spanish. For the most part, it appeared the students were completing worksheets, which couldn't be good for kids in any language.

She was glad when that class ended and she was able to enter the cool courtyard and take in some sunshine before lunch. The high school kids got a morning break of fifteen minutes, just enough time to socialize and process before the next class.

Roughly a hundred of the kids had decided to spend their break outside in the beautiful courtyard between the middle and high school buildings. It looked more like a park in an upscale planned community than something one would find on school grounds. Evergreen plants and seasonal blooms brought color to the setting. Tiffany could only imagine what this place might look like in the spring. Hopefully, she'd be there to find out.

Kids clumped in groups, talking to one another. She recognized the cliques from her high school days: the nerds, the jocks, the mean girls, the goths, the free-spirits.

She spotted Braxton walking toward her bench. It took every ounce of holiness in her to keep from imagining his jacket falling to the concrete, his shirt magically unbuttoning against the cool November winds, revealing the chest she'd gotten a pretty good outline of in that t-shirt he'd worn to her mother's house. *Is he going to look this good every single day? And am I going to act so brand new every time?*

He casually sat next to her. "Sup?"

Tiffany steadied her breath. "Just checking out the

cliques. Not much has changed."

He surveyed the crowd. "Where are the comedians?"

"I don't know. I guess in the principal's office 'cause that's where class clowns usually end up."

"Awwww, why you gotta talk about my people like that?"

All the groups of boys did an about-face, looking toward Tiffany's left. She followed their line of sight to find Deja looking like a runway model in her skin-tight black dress with a peek-a-boo chest cutout and six-inch heels.

Made Tiffany feel like she'd come to work in a pair of pajamas, wearing a simple black pantsuit and flats.

"Hey. How are my two favorite nemesises?"

Braxton looked at Tiffany like *is-that-a-word*?

Deja sat on the other side of Braxton. "Got your game plan together for the final pitch?"

"I'm good," Braxton answered.

Deja eyed Tiffany.

"Same here. You?"

Deja said, "Yep. This school needs a lot of help. I went to that forensics class. Oh. My. Gosh. That guy does *nothing*! Those kids are *teaching themselves*! He gotta go. Whew! And I'm so glad today's over with. Being around all these kids is driving me insane. They're so...energetic. And all this praying! At a *school*! Who does that?"

Tiffany remained silent, secretly hoping Deja

would repeat those words *verbatim* in her presentation. She'd talk herself right out of the runnings.

The rant continued, "I can't. This school needs to stop resembling a compound and start preparing kids for the *real* world ahead. Oh, and don't even get me started on that funky agricultural building. All those ratchet farm animals. Smells like the zoo." Deja shimmied her shoulders.

A knot tightened inside Tiffany's stomach. *The agricultural building.* She'd all but forgotten this last leg of her journey.

Deja bumped herself against Braxton. "You want to compare notes later?"

"No." He offered no courtesy.

Tiffany stifled an all-out guffaw.

"Don't be a poor sport. Iron sharpens iron, right? Isn't that somewhere in the Bible?"

"As a matter of fact, it is."

"See, I'm not a *total* heathen, Mr. Braxton Stoneworth."

Tiffany didn't like the way his name dripped from Deja's lips. Downright nasty.

"Correct," Braxton agreed sarcastically. "You should come to our women's Bible study. I think you'd benefit. My mom leads it."

"Oh." She threw her shoulders back. "You want me to meet your mother?"

"All for the Lord's glory."

Her shoulder's slumped. She snuck a peek at

Tiffany. "What do you think? Was that an invitation to meet his mom?"

"I think it was more an invitation to meet Jesus," Tiffany answered. When she saw Deja's outrage, Tiffany felt convicted and quickly added, "On a deeper level, I mean. We could all use a closer walk with Him. Right, Braxton?"

Braxton covered his mouth, failing at an attempt to hide his amusement. "Mmm hmm."

"Well, I can't get to the Bible study any time soon. I've got classes in the evenings. Working on my M-B-A."

"Good for you," Tiffany congratulated sincerely. "The degree will serve you well."

"Yeah, well, I gotta go do some more reading for my class as well as get ready for the teacher interviews. Toodles," she waved distinctively and solely at Braxton.

"I need to pray," Braxton told Tiffany as soon as Deja walked out of hearing distance.

"Why?"

"This woman got my phone number from Rhonda. Called me twice last night and sent me a picture of herself in attire that was...let's say...something one would wear to bed. With a spouse. On a honeymoon."

"No! For real?" Tiffany held her hand out for his phone.

Braxton pushed her nubs away. "I'm not going to show you the picture. That would be...unmanly."

Tiffany raised an eyebrow. "But you haven't *deleted* it."

"No. I might need it for blackmail if push comes to shove with this deal."

"Really?"

"No." Braxton laughed. "Of course I deleted it. You think *I'm* the heathen here?"

"Well, it would be quite unmanly of you get rid of a picture of a beautiful woman."

He scratched the back of his neck. "I won't lie. I thought about keeping it. But she's not the one I want on my mind."

Tiffany's stomach liquefied.

"In other news, are you ready for the agricultural building?" he asked.

"Never."

"It's now or never. And it's not as bad as Deja said. I mean, it does stink and all…but the animals aren't ratchet."

The knot pulled tighter. "You remember why I don't do animals, right?" She pointed at the scar on her left calf, the constant reminder of what happened the day she went to visit cousins, Chrystal and Lorenzo. They had rescued a dog a month earlier from the shelter. Both her cousins and her aunt assured Tiffany beyond the shadow of doubt that Fee-Fee didn't bite.

Sure enough, when Tiffany put her leg out there for Fee-Fee to lick, the dog took a chunk out of Tiffany's calf. The blood, the screams, the pain, the needle, the stitches. And she later learned that the dog was put to sleep. *Dead because of me.*

"Yes, I remember," he said. "I'm going to tell you the truth: anything with teeth can bite. The trick is to approach animals gently, but without fear."

"I put my leg out there *gently* for Fee-Fee," Tiffany recalled nervously.

"Look, Fee-Fee had a flashback," Braxton joked. "Maybe her previous owner used to kick her or something."

"Well, I'm having the flashback now," Tiffany said, not swayed by his humor.

"Don't worry. I already saved you once from a piglet."

Tiffany rolled her eyes at him. "Let's get this over with." Animals. Pigs, chickens, dogs and rabbits. Tiffany was glad she hadn't eaten lunch yet.

They walked to the dreaded building. She stopped near the entrance. The smells had already assaulted her nose and she was still ten feet from the wood.

Braxton whispered from behind, "You going to walk inside?"

"Do I have to?"

"Yes, if you want to experience it."

"I *don't* want to."

"You have to. Come on." He grabbed her hand and led her down the main aisle of the barn. The animal odor worsened as they progressed into the building. Tiffany used her jacket to shield her nose.

All around them were students of various ages,

along with three adults caring for the creatures. Feeding, washing, even playing with them.

I hope they get good baths right after school, Tiffany thought.

"Keep walking," Braxton prodded when her feet seemed to quit at the sight of a German Shepherd on their path. It wasn't quite an adult, but still...it had teeth and a mind of its own.

"He's looking at us," Tiffany said, trying to keep her lips from moving.

"Yes. He's a shepherd, that's what they do."

"Let's go look at the rabbits. Do rabbits have teeth?"

"Yes, but they're not known for biting."

For some reason, Tiffany thought about Bugs Bunny's huge teeth. She almost mentioned him but caught herself before voicing this irrational fear.

You can do this, girl. You got this.

She allowed Braxton to lead her to the rabbit's pen, where an older teen was busy raking the cage.

"Hi," the boy said.

"Hey," Braxton responded. "We just want to look at the little ones."

"Over there." He pointed to the back corner of the enclosure.

Tiffany's throat tightened. She allowed Braxton to proceed first.

He bent down and picked up the smallest rabbit in the bunch, arguably just a ball of white fur. Slowly, he stepped toward her.

Fee-Fee was slow, too.

Tiffany shuffled back.

"Tiff, this is a baby. He's only got four teeth. And they're small."

"Okay. Thank you. You can put it back now."

"I think he likes you," Braxton came closer.

"Put that thing down."

Suddenly, she felt something brush against her foot. In panic, she rushed into Braxton's arms. The baby rabbit squirmed between them flat against her chest.

"Oh my gosh!" Tiffany shrieked.

Somehow, as both she and Braxton tried to get away from one another and the killer rabbit at her feet, the tiny rabbit began to fall.

Instinctively, Tiffany caught the fur ball before it could meet an untimely death.

"Take it, Braxton! Take it!" she screamed, thrusting it toward him.

He stepped away. "You got it, Tiff. You're holding it. It's okay," he coaxed.

Tiff panted and stared down into her own hands. He was right. She was holding an animal in her hands. A tiny animal, but still—a furry creature with four legs and teeth.

The rabbit seemed to wave with its whiskers.

She blubbered, "I'm holding it! I'm holding it, Braxton!" Despite her awkward posture—legs apart, arms thrust completely forward, bent at the waist—she was excited for this small accomplishment.

"Yes, you are!" He whipped out his phone. "Let me take a picture, for the record."

He snapped one with her holding the animal. For the second picture, he helped her assume a more natural pose, still keeping the bunny far enough from her face for comfort. Braxton came behind her to took a selfie of the two of them with the baby rabbit.

Then he relieved her of Baby Bugs and placed the animal with its peeps.

"That was crazy." Tiffany shivered, wiping her hands against her thighs as they left the rabbit section and walked toward the exit.

"You did it. You actually touched an animal."

"Send me that picture. None of my friends will believe it," she squeaked.

They continued toward the main building, both glued to their phones – Braxton sending and Tiffany receiving, resending the pictures. Almost instantly, her friends replied—not about the rabbit but about Braxton.

CASSIE: Who is he?

MONICE: Is that the preacher's kid? He fyner than on streaming video

TYRA: Ask him about his brother.

Tiffany replied to all: What about ME and the RABBIT?!!!

MONICE: Silly rabbit, tricks are for kids. We need info about the MAN.

Tiffany busted out laughing.

"What?" Braxton asked.

Tiffany put the phone away. "My friends are wild."

Chapter 13

The after-school interviews with teachers were quite intense. Tiffany asked a series of questions aimed at determining the team leaders' willingness and aptitude for supervising and developing others. She knew from experience that the person who does something best isn't always the person who develops capacity in others best. It seemed like... perhaps Mr. McDonald and his team had selected the teachers with the highest test scores as department chairs.

When she started working with them, her first order of business would have to be reselecting team leads, and that wouldn't go over well, especially considering that there was a significant stipend for team leaders.

But this was her domain. This was what she did. This was what people paid her to do—analyze data, push feelings aside, get the job done. The culture was important, of course, and so were people. But productivity with integrity was the bottom line for Mr. McDonald, and Tiffany was excited about the possible chance to help him reach that goal.

She finished six interviews in ninety minutes. After which, she met with Mr. McDonald's secretary to schedule her pitch for Monday. That's when it would all go down.

Tiffany checked out with Rhonda, then walked to her car with ideas spinning in her head. The sheer challenge of this project was energizing.

She spotted Braxton standing at her car. Resisted the urge to kiss him on school property. "Hey there. How'd your interviews go?"

"Well," he said, although his face showed distress.

"What's the matter?"

"Okay, so now I have a favor to ask you."

"Anything."

"My daughter's turning eight next week. I was thinking about getting Brianna her own personal bowling ball, but her mother says that's not a good idea.

Tiffany waited a second for his smile—*he had to be joking, right?*

Yet his tight lips revealed that he was dead serious.

"Is she in a bowling league?"

"No. Just something she might want to do one day."

Tiffany coughed away a laugh. "Yeah, I'm going to have to agree with her mother. You should get something else. Girls love clothes. A doll, maybe. Are her ears pierced?"

Braxton gave a pitiful shrug.

Tiffany sighed. "All right. Let's do this."

This time, Braxton followed Tiffany to her side of town. The best shopping to be had was in her neighborhood. Tiffany texted ahead to her fifteen-year-old niece, Madison, who cleaned Tiffany's apartment on Thursdays. Tiffany didn't really need a housekeeper, but she employed her niece in order to indirectly help her sister, financially.

TIFFANY: Make sure the place is tidy. Toilet paper, towel in bathroom. Got company.
MADISON: Who?
TIFFANY: Stay out of grown folks biznes

Their first stop was at a Coat Factory that sold a lot more than coats.

"Do you know what size she wears?"

"No. She wore a 6X last year."

"I'm pretty sure she doesn't wear a 6X anymore," Tiffany said. "Kids grow up fast." *How long has it been since he's seen his own child?* "You got a picture of her?"

Braxton swiped through his phone, then held up a shot of the little girl with big brown eyes and long, thick braids. "She's so cute!"

"Thanks."

Tiffany enlarged the photo. "Okay. She's standing next to her teacher's desk, that gives me some idea of her height. She's pretty slim. I think we'll be safe with a size 8 in something that'll be appropriate for the winter through spring. That way if it's too big, she can grow into it."

Braxton sucked his neck in. "I'm impressed."

"I've got sisters and nieces, remember? As a matter of fact, my niece Madison is probably at my house now. She cleans for me on Thursdays after school."

"Cool."

"Now, if we can't find an outfit, we'll move on to toys. Does she like dolls?"

"Pshhh, I don't know."

It was one thing for him to be unclear about the child's size. But why didn't he know what his daughter's interests were? *Is Braxton a deadbeat dad?* If the answer to that question was "yes", Tiffany would have to throw this brother back into the sea.

They shopped for an hour, picking up a sweater jacket with a furry collar in the coat store and a girly bath and body pack. They could, at least, be sure she took baths.

Though Tiffany tried to enjoy her time with Braxton, she couldn't shake the questions in her mind about the type of father he was to Brianna. If the Stoneworths were all that, surely they taught their men better than to ditch paternal responsibilities.

Tiffany had grown up with a great father, but most of her friends hadn't, and she'd seen the havoc it caused in their relationships with men as well as the Lord. She wouldn't settle for anything less than a good man for her own future children, if motherhood was in her future.

At the register in their final store, where they'd picked up bracelets and a matching necklace, Braxton

139

threw in a container of lip gloss.

"Is her mom letting her wear lip gloss yet?" Tiffany asked, though by this time she was fed up with his inability to answer questions.

"Lip gloss is a rite of passage?"

"Yes. It is."

Braxton argued, "Isn't it basically the same thing as putting Vaseline on your lips?"

"Yes and no," Tiffany explained. "When you put on lip gloss, you're using the same motions as putting on lipstick. You're training her for what she'll do when she gets older. Some moms don't allow lip gloss for a while. Besides, it's much shinier than Vaseline." She put the gloss back in its display holder

"Man, I've got a lot to learn."

"Your dad played football, but from what I remember, he was still pretty strict. Might as well have been a preacher back then, too. I know there was stuff you couldn't do that made no sense to you."

"Yeah," Braxton recalled, "I remember I couldn't eat candy cigarettes or drink from those little wax beer cans."

"Same philosophy. I'm not saying it's right, just clarifying it."

"So you think it's wrong to eat candy cigarettes?"

Tiffany thought out loud, "I mean, on one hand, it's only candy. But on the other hand, if we're training kids up in the way we want them to go and that's *not* the way we want them to go, why practice it?"

Braxton nodded. "I like you, girl. But I still like candy cigarettes."

"Why eat the candy cigarettes when you can get Fun-Dip? Those are much bigger and they taste better, plus you get the flavored powder!"

"Now, that's what's up," Braxton stamped his approval. He stole a kiss from her lips.

Tiffany prayed her knees wouldn't give out from sudden weakness.

After they finished shopping, Tiffany and Braxton grabbed a bite to eat at the mall's food court.

"I really appreciate you helping me with my daughter. It's hard when we live so far apart."

"Oh? I thought you said you'd taught her fractions?"

"Virtually," Braxton clarified. "She lives with her mother in Chicago. You might remember her mom from Pinkston. Alicia Williams?"

The name didn't ring a bell. "No."

"She enrolled our sophomore year."

"Did she finish college?"

"No. She's got a good job, though. I've wanted to see Brianna more often, but different things have come up. Plus I couldn't drive anywhere with the license suspension. Man, that was hard. I don't know what I would have done without my family."

Tiffany couldn't believe she was having this conversation with a guy. She always stayed clear of people with records of any kind. Better safe than sorry. On the other hand, she was glad to know that distance and circumstances played a part in why he seemed so unaware of his daughter's likes and dislikes. If his actions today were any indication, Braxton was determined to fix things with his daughter.

Optimistically, she asked, "Would her mother consider flying Brianna here to see you?"

Braxton slurped his Coke. "Maybe, when she's older, we'd both feel comfortable putting her on a flight by herself."

"I see."

His somber expression was painful to watch. Tiffany couldn't remember seeing him so grave. So serious. His concern for his daughter touched her heart. *He's a good man after all.*

"Her mother is familiar with my old ways. I think she's afraid, until she knows I'm stable. The D-U-I didn't help. I'm hoping to turn some things around with steady work, you know?"

"Same here," Tiffany said. "My family's counting on me to step in. Help my mom while she's grieving."

"Aren't you grieving, too?"

"Yeah, but...my family...even though I'm the baby girl, it's like I'm the big sister to everyone, my mother included. I asked God for strength to deal with it all."

Braxton countered, "They're all grown, Tiff. They can learn to depend on God for what they need just like everybody else."

"I know," she agreed. "My dad. He spoiled us

all."

"I wouldn't say he spoiled you. I'd say he showed you what it was like to be able to depend on someone. Nothing wrong with him being a good example, giving you a glimpse of how good God is."

Tiffany squinted at Braxton. "You are so on point when it comes to spiritual matters. I can't imagine you *not* preaching. You make more sense than a lot of the people I hear on television."

He chuckled. "Let me get this D-U-I off my back first."

Oh yeah. That.

After the meal, they headed back to their cars.

"You got wrapping paper?" Tiffany checked.

Braxton bleated, "No. You didn't say anything about wrapping paper."

"You need to wrap it up before you mail it. If you don't, her mother's going to have to wrap it when she gets it – more work on her."

Braxton sighed. "All these unspoken expectations."

"It's only a matter of logistics. By the way, do you know how to wrap a gift?"

"No. I usually get a gift bag. Ain't nobody got time for scissors and tape and all that."

"Well, a gift bag that won't work because you've got to mail it." Tiffany tsked him. "Come on. Follow me home. I've got plenty of pink wrapping paper there."

"Ugh. You people..." he said, shaking his head.

As Braxton followed, Tiffany called ahead to let her niece that she was almost home and would have company.

"Who is it?" Madison wanted to know.

"Uh, stay out of grown folks business."

Chapter 14

Braxton seemed all-too-excited to follow her into her abode. Tiffany jangled her keys at the door. "Why are you so happy?"

""Cause I get to see the truth. They say who you are at home is who you are."

Tiffany opened the door to her apartment wide, letting Braxton in behind her. The simple, clean lines, white walls, and hardwood floors always brought a sense of calm when she entered her home.

Braxton poked out his lips as though inspecting her quarters. "Not too shabby."

"Whatever. Come on in so we can hook your daughter up."

Madison bounded from the kitchen wearing a PINK Hoodie, skinny jeans, and an inquiring glance. "Hey, Auntie!"

The ladies hugged. "Madison, this is my friend, Braxton. Braxton, my niece, Madison."

"Nice to meet you," he shook her hand.

"Same here."

"You clean up for your aunt every week?"

"Yes, sir."

"How long does it take?"

Tiffany slapped his arm. "Don't be quizzing my niece for dirt. She's on my side, right Maddi?"

"Yep." She slid into Tiffany's waist.

"You finished cleaning?"

"Everything except your room. I'm working on it now."

"Don't let us hold you up."

Madison left them alone to finish her work. Tiffany led Braxton to the kitchen table. "Take everything out. Take off the prices, but try to leave on the barcodes in case they need to return something. I'll be right back."

She left Braxton in the kitchen while she searched for boxes in her office closet. She found the perfect sizes – a smaller one to contain the gifts, the next size up to serve as the mailer.

When she returned to the kitchen, she found Braxton snooping in her nearly-bare refrigerator.

"What are you doing?"

"Do you eat in here?"

"No, I do not eat in my refrigerator."

"I mean in this house." He motioned toward the unencumbered countertops. "No mixer, no toaster, no canisters. How do you cook?"

"I don't. I can't. It's not my thing."

Braxton's head rolled from side to side. "Tragic."

"There's no reason to cook every day. It's just me, and there are plenty of healthy restaurants in the area. I might spend six bucks on a salad that lasts me two meals. Works for me."

"Well, it ain't gonna work for me. The woman I settle down with has got to burn in the kitchen."

"Good for her," Tiffany sassed.

Braxton closed the refrigerator.

Tiffany tried to put his rude comment out of her mind. *Think of the child.*

Braxton joined her at the table. "I'm sorry. I didn't mean to insult you in your own house."

Tiffany let him off the hook with, "No worries. My dad used to fuss at me for not taking an interest in cooking. I just never caught on. Why do you think I made you a sandwich yesterday at my mom's?"

"Mmmmm," Braxton said. "Well, it was a delicious sandwich."

"Thank you."

With that behind them, Tiffany and Braxton proceeded with the gift-wrapping session. When he thoroughly messed up the first flap, Tiffany narrowed his involvement to one task.

"Braxton, step away from the box. All I want you to do is give me tape strips."

He raised his hands and allowed Tiffany the front seat with this gift.

"No problem," he hummed.

She demonstrated. "You tuck the insides. Then you press the top and bottom into triangles, like so."

Braxton swooped in from behind her and put his hands over hers. "Walk me through it again." His body heat permeated through her sweater.

Try as she might, Tiffany couldn't stop the butterflies from dancing in her stomach as Braxton pretended to learn the fine art of wrapping paper while practicing the age-old art of flirting.

With the first corner securely in place, he kissed her cheek.

The kiss right there—the overhead swoop-down—was a treasure. Not many men were tall enough to kiss *down* her face. His lips sent a rush of heat clear to her feet.

She turned her body to face him, threw her arms over his shoulders, and pulled him in for a kiss that took her further than she'd meant to go, longer than she'd meant to stay. Sheer electricity awakened desires Tiffany hadn't even known existed as Braxton gently, but expertly, commandeered through their most intimate kiss yet. He drew her closer, her body molding to his.

Tiffany had been kissed before—but never like this. And never to the point where she thought she might actually suffocate, in a good way.

"Ummm...excuse me. Auntie?"

Tiffany and Braxton jumped. Arms fell to their sides.

Tiffany readjusted her shirt. She cleared her throat. "Yes, Maddi, what is it?"

Madison's eyes were round with wonder. "I was gonna ask if you wanted me to switch out the rugs in your bathroom."

"Okay," Tiffany exhaled. "Yes. That would be great."

Madison pulled the trigger on an imaginary gun. "Gotcha." She walked out of the kitchen.

"She did get you," Braxton said.

Tiffany slapped his arm. "She got you, too!"

"Yeah, but she's not going to tell my mother."

"True. We'd better wrap these gifts and keep it moving."

Tiffany's phone buzzed three times. She ignored each one, anxious to complete the job and get Braxton out of her apartment before they got locked in another too-hot-to-handle situation. *If Madison hadn't been here, what would have happened?*

Tiffany gave herself a little credit, reminding herself that she never would have invited Braxton into her place alone to begin with. She hadn't been in any serious relationships, but still—you don't get to be a twenty-eight-year-old virgin in the twenty-first century by accident. Aside from being committed to Christ and married to work, Tiffany was no stranger to staging her way around temptation.

"The hard work is done," Tiffany said as she placed a smaller box inside the larger one. She handed them both to Braxton. "Now all you have to do is tape the outer box, address it, and send it in the mail. Think you can take it from here?"

"Yep." He stole another kiss. "Thank you."

Tiffany recovered from the shivers. "You're welcome."

She picked up her phone, since whoever this was obviously had a problem with this fourth text. The texts had come from her oldest sister.

5:58 TERRI ANNE: Ummm...hello? Why is

there some strange dude in the house with my daughter?

6:15 TERRI ANNE: Why are you kissing in front of Maddi?

6:17 TERRI ANNE: Do you know how hard it is to raise a kid these days without my own sister, her favorite aunt, setting a dad example???

6:20 TERRI ANNE: Never mind. I'll be on my way to get her as soon as I get off work before you show her something else I don't want her to see.

Tiffany's mouth fell to the floor. "Really?"

"What?" Braxton asked, leaning over her shoulder to look at the screen.

Tiffany blackened the screen. "My sister. Apparently, my niece told her that we kissed. And now she's having a cow."

Braxton ventured, "Is she unaware that you're an adult?"

"My sister's fourteen years older than me. She still thinks I'm twelve. Except for when she calls to ask for money, then I'm sixty," Tiffany spouted off more than she should have. *Forgive me, Lord.*

"Let me go clear this up with my niece."

Tiffany walked to her bedroom, knocked on her own door. "Maddi?"

"Yes, Auntie?"

"Sweetheart. Come here." Tiffany sat on her bed and patted a spot next to her.

Maddi, confused, obeyed. "What's going on?"

"Sweetheart, I didn't mean to set a bad example by kissing Braxton."

"What?"

"Well, your mom is pretty upset about—"

"Oh my gosh! It was only a kiss! I told her how great it was to see you with somebody! I had no idea she would turn it into drama!"

Maddi, who was drama rolled into a hundred-pound body, quickly drew tears to her eyes. "I'm sorry. I didn't mean to get my mom mad at you. I thought she would be happy for you."

Tiffany hugged her niece. "It's okay, honey. I just want to be clear with you." After several seconds, she pushed Madison back a bit. Holding onto the girl's shoulders, Tiffany stated, "Number one, I never intended for you to see that kiss. Number two, I want you know there's a difference between children and adults. And number three, most importantly, we *all* have to remember that God is a witness to everything we do at *any* age.

"I don't make it a habit of bringing men to my apartment. But Braxton is...special to me," Tiffany admitted to herself as well. "He and I have known each other since I was in college. I know kissing may not seem like a big deal to you and your friends, but it *is* an intimate gesture. Not something I suggest you do with every guy you meet."

Madison's gaze dropped to the floor.

"Maddi, have you been kissing someone?"

She muttered, "No. But everyone I know has. In a

151

way, I want to. But I don't know how. Or who. Plus it seems kinda gross." Madison swung her head up. "Did you know that kissing someone is equivalent to licking their plate after they've eaten?"

"Eeeew! That's nasty!" Tiffany considered, covering her mouth.

"Yep. It is. That's another reason I haven't kissed anybody yet. I don't like other people's germs."

"Yes. Which is why you're such a great housekeeper." Tiffany walked to her bathroom. "I'm gonna need some mouthwash."

Madison rolled off the bed laughing. "You got cooties!"

"I sure do." Tiffany swished the blue liquid between her teeth and over her gums before spitting into the sink. "Now, call your mom back and tell her not to worry about coming all the way across town to get you in the middle of rush hour traffic. I'll bring you home like I always do."

"Yes, ma'am."

Tiffany left her niece to finish cleaning.

Braxton was sitting at the end of the couch in her living room, perusing through a book.

"I need you to stop going rambling through my belongings every time I leave the room," she fussed, sitting on the other stool.

"Technically, since I am *in* the book, I have a vested interest in this property."

Tiffany looked down and realized that he was flipping through their sophomore yearbook from

Pinkston College.

He plopped his finger on a picture of Tiffany dribbling down the basketball court. Skinny as a beanpole, hair in braids pulled back into a ponytail.

She moved his finger. "Stop."

"I'm so glad you got some meat on your bones," he teased. "Although you didn't actually *cook* the meat..."

"Anyway!" She shoved him. "Let me find a picture of *you*." She flipped quickly to the section highlighting fraternities and sororities. "Bam! Right here!" She slapped the page showing Braxton and his brothers flashing their hand signals in notorious poses. They all looked drunk in that picture.

Braxton said, "Man, we were all wasted when they snapped that shot."

"I was just about to comment to that effect."

They continued the walk down memory lane, stopping to laugh about old teachers and classmates. Braxton informed her of a few people who had passed—one died in a car accident, another lost a battle to cancer. But for the most part, everyone seemed to be doing well. Braxton had humorous anecdotes galore, which Tiffany enjoyed hearing.

When they got to the freshman section, Tiffany pointed to a girl and jabbered, "Oh my gosh, this girl right here! She was in my suite. Had a different guy in her room every week, and she *never* got caught. I wanted to tell on her 'cause I was kinda scared to go the bathroom sometimes with all those different dudes around, but my roommate didn't want to snitch. I don't even remember this girl's real name. We started calling her T-L-C cause that girl could *creep*. Wonder what ever happened to her?"

Tiffany looked up at Braxton.

He face was stone.

"You know her?"

"Yeah. She's Brianna's mother."

Tiffany nearly choked on her own breath. "Oh. I'm sorry."

A vein popped out and pulsed at Braxton's temple.

Tiffany backpedaled, "I'm sure she's a very good mother. People *can* change, you know?"

Braxton parked a closed fist over his mouth. "She is."

"That's good," Tiffany agreed nervously, wishing she'd never opened her big mouth.

"So let me ask you something."

Tiffany gulped.

"You think Brianna might not be mine?"

Tiffany shrugged innocently. "There's always a *chance*."

His countenance darkened in disappointment.

"But she *does* have dimples like you, Braxton. She *could be* yours. Why didn't you do a D-N-A test?"

"Alicia's out of state. Lot of paperwork. I didn't even know I had a daughter the first two years. And then she sent the pictures and my mom was like,

'Braxton, that's yours.' So I stopped questioning myself." He traced the top of the box intended for Brianna. "But I'm sitting here looking through this book with you, looking at all the faces. All the dudes she could have been with, thinking—wonder if *this* guy is really Brianna's dad. And then you said what you said. Made me question again."

"Are you paying child support?" Tiffany asked.

"Not through the courts. Alicia and I agreed to a set amount every month and I send it. It's kind of a good thing, too, because when I got arrested and had to give my dad money for the legal fees, I got behind. I was able to catch up eventually, but had I been court-ordered, I would have probably found myself behind bars again."

Tiffany plopped her chin in her palm. Perhaps she had watched one too many Maury Povich shows back in the day, but she'd heard that story one too many times. The women who didn't want to go through the courts either wanted the man back or didn't want the truth to come to light. "You should do the D-N-A test, Braxton."

He rubbed his waves roughly. "Man, I can't do this right now. Brianna helps me keep focused. Gives me something to work toward, you know? Don't distract me like this."

"I'm not trying to distract you. But if she isn't your daughter, you need to know. *She* deserves to know. If she is, great. But if she isn't...maybe that would take away some of the pressure. You might

155

even consider preaching again, since you insist that being a single dad is another strike in your life."

Braxton's face puffed up. He blew the air out slowly. "I feel like you're taking me out of my game plan."

"What game plan?"

"To get this contract and get my life together. Is that what you're doing? You sure you didn't already know Alicia was Brianna's mom?"

Tiffany gave him the stank-eye and replied, "I don't have to cheat in order to beat you."

Anger burned across Braxton's countenance. "I wouldn't put it past you. You've always been competitive."

Tiffany threw her hands in the air. "Are you kidding me right now?"

"Naw. I think I'd better leave."

"Fine!"

Chapter 15

Braxton's insides boiled with indignation as he grabbed the wrapped gifts from the kitchen table. He knew Alicia was no saint—none of the girls who pursued the Lambdas were—but Tiffany had gone out of her way to paint the mother of his child as a straight-up male version of himself. His *old* self. Ridiculous. No woman could be that bad.

He tucked Brianna's box under his arm and pulled his keys from his pockets. He threw a few dollars from his wallet onto Tiffany's kitchen bar. "For the wrapping paper."

"Keep it. I don't want anything from you."

"No, I don't want anything from you."

"Fine," she said, stuffing the money in her pocket. "My momma didn't raise no fool."

Tiffany's cell phone rang as she escorted him to the door.

He stepped aside to let her handle the locks. She unlatched the first, but froze in conversation "What? Wait! What are you talking about?"

Alarmed, Braxton. Despite his anger, he wanted to make sure Tiffany wasn't facing an emergency.

"No! I didn't get a call from you yesterday!" She paused. "No. I was at my mother's…I…hold on."

She scrolled through her phone. Stopped suddenly. Sighed and returned to the conversation.

"Yes, I see your number in my call log, but I—"

The person on the other line's voice gained volume, though Braxton couldn't make out the words.

"Yes. I understand. I apologize. Because I missed the call, it went to voice mail. And I don't normally check my voice mail unless I realize I've missed a...yes. I understand...yes. I'll send my final invoice tomorrow."

Tiffany muttered, "Great," under her breath as she opened the door.

"Are you okay?" Braxton asked, hoping she wouldn't start crying. If Tiffany broke down, he wasn't sure how he'd be able to stay angry.

"Ugh! I missed a call...a very important call. Missed the voice mail that came along with it. My biggest client had a major change, scheduled an emergency meeting for today, and I knew nothing about it. They've released me from the project." She tapped through the screen. "Six forty-nine. Yesterday. Wait. Braxton, we were in the car together at six forty-nine yesterday. How did I miss this call?"

Braxton remembered. His stomach sank. "You were sound asleep. I shut off the ringer—"

"You did what?!" she raged, her eyes hooded with anger. "You had no right! Braxton, I'm a one-woman business. I can't afford to miss calls! I don't have a dad to fall back on like some people! And you have the *nerve* to accuse me of trying to sabotage *you*? Pleeeeze!"

Her eyes filled with tears. "Get out."

"Tiff, I honestly forgot to tell you."

She opened the door wider. Her chin trembled. "Just leave."

Braxton's humor couldn't save him this time. Nor could reasoning, apparently. With his own anger still simmering, too, he thought it best to follow Tiffany's advice.

Not wanting to upset her niece, Tiffany holed up in the guest bathroom for a minute to collect herself. Her hands were still shaking. Breath still short. He had cost her a job. Her rent. Not to mention her heart. Again. *How could I have been so stupid?*

The doorbell rang. *He is really pushing it.* But if he wanted more of the hard truth, she would certainly let him have it!

Tiffany stomped to the door and swung it open, ready to go another round with Braxton.

"Hello." Terri Anne rolled her neck, her Senegalese twists bouncing with the movement.

Tiffany shifted her weight to one side. "I told you I would bring Maddi home."

"Too late. I was already on my way. What's wrong with you? You been crying?" She stepped inside the apartment and closed the door, then took off walking around the apartment before Tiffany could answer. "You should be crying, after what you did in front of Maddie. She's fifteen. Fighting hormones. And here you are giving her lessons on

159

how to lose control of 'em," Terri Anne rambled, peeking around corners.

Tiffany stood fixed at the door, waiting for her sister to stop yapping.

Terri Anne must have finally noticed that she was talking to herself. She came back to the living area and stood. For the first time, the leather boots ceased clomping in search of the guest who had already left. "You just gonna stand there?"

Tiffany combed her hair back with her fingers. "Maddie is in my room." She closed the front door.

"Aren't you going to apologize?" Terri Anne approached her again. "And what's wrong with you? You feeling okay?" She placed the back of her hand on Tiffany's forehead, checking for a temperature.

Tiffany yanked away. "You always thought you were my mother."

"I might as well have been. Momma made me take you to games so I wouldn't get pregnant," Terri Anne recalled. "Maybe that's what Maddie needs. Somebody to tag along."

The very thought almost made Tiffany laugh as she realized that's exactly what she'd done with Madison earlier—used the girl as a means to keep the apartment off-limits for slip-ups.

"I'm fine. Had a little argument with Braxton."

"Oh. Is that his name?" Terri Anne folded her arms. "He the one who fixed up Momma's house yesterday?"

"News travels fast."

"Mmm hmm. You'd better be careful."

"Terri Anne, I'm twenty-eight years old. I'm not a baby," Tiffany defended herself.

"Maddie! Come on! We gotta go!" Terri called toward Tiffany's bedroom.

"Okay! In a minute."

Terri tightened the belt on her trench coat. "You pay Momma's cable bill?"

"No. I don't think I'll be able to," Tiffany admitted reluctantly, thinking of the contract she'd just lost. "Things are getting tight around here. You think maybe you and Tina could help with some bills?"

"I'm a single mother," Terri Ann blasted, "I don't have any extra money. I didn't get to go to college."

Here we go again. "You could have."

"Says the girl who was Daddy's favorite."

Now it was Tiffany's turn to cross her arms as she faced her sister. Braxton's liberating words of advice flew back to her. *They can learn to depend on God for what they need just like everybody else.* "You know what? Momma doesn't have to have cable. The only reason they had it at the house was because of Daddy and all his sports channels. If no one else wants to pay for it, we can have it disconnected. She wouldn't care one way or another."

"But when our kids go over to stay with her, what will they watch?" Terri Anne asked.

"If you and Tina want your kids to have cable at Momma's, you two should pay for it." *That felt good.*

"Another thing, I know Daddy always handled the bills, but Momma's not illiterate. She can learn how to budget and take care of herself." Tiffany was on a roll. "One more thing, this Christmas we need to draw names. I can't go broke trying to buy for everybody's kids. We need to make these family finances and responsibilities more equitable."

"But you're the only one with a college degree, a decent job and no kids," Terri Anne fussed. "We all sacrificed so you could earn that paper!"

"How exactly did you sacrifice, Terri Ann? You were, like, thirty-five when I went to college."

"Daddy cut us off when you went to school. He was always talking about how he had to pay something on Tiff's tuition, pay for Tiff's room and board, pay for Tiff's books," Terri Anne mimicked their father's voice. "It was only by the grace of God that I've been able to keep Maddie clothed and fed all by myself!"

"I can't even feel sorry for you," Tiffany said. "At least you had Daddy until you were almost forty. I'm twenty-eight and I'm having to lean completely on God alone a lot sooner than you did. But I ain't mad. A friend told me that God's even more faithful than a good earthly father. I have to believe that now." Tiffany's voice wavered with sentiment. "We all do, 'cause I can't fill Willie Dale Warren's shoes."

Terri Anne reached out to hug Tiffany.

Over these last months, Tiffany had been holding up for the family. Not today. She allowed herself to sink into Terri Anne's arms and cry like the little sister she'd never been allowed to become.

Tiffany felt Madison embrace her from the backside. "It's okay, Auntie."

Sandwiched between her older sister and younger niece, Tiffany succumbed to their circle of love.

Madison added, "Don't worry. You'll find another man."

"What?" Tiffany and Terri Anne broke the group hug.

"Isn't that what we're crying about?"

"Girl, no!" Terri Anne hollered playfully. "We're crying over your grandpa. And some changes we need to make in this family."

"Oh. Okay." Madison pulled her mother and aunt back in. "Either way, it's going to be all right."

Finally, with the place to herself again, Tiffany flopped on the couch and replayed the day's arguments. Braxton. Terri Anne. The Hillman account. Braxton Terri Anne. The names swirled around in her head, almost making her dizzy with confusion. Did Braxton have a right to be angry? Was Terri Ann overreacting?

Unable to make sense of it all, Tiffany fell to her knees and invited God into the discussion. "Lord, this has been an awful evening. I messed up with Braxton. I think. But I don't know what I could have done differently?"

She stopped mid-breath as she sensed another replay. This time, her mental tape rewound to the moment before she began to talk about Alicia. Braxton was so humorous, always entertaining. She had thought this was her opportunity to make him laugh, too. With gossip.

Gossip. The word weighed heavy on her heart.

She released it to Him in confession, "Father, I repent of using gossip as a form of entertainment when You have called it sin and slander. Thank You for a spirit of repentance, and thank You, Jesus, for forgiveness."

Next, she prayed about the situation with Terri Anne and Madison. "God, You know I don't want to be a bad example for my niece. Help me to be mindful of my sister's job as a mother. And help me to keep my hands off Braxton. Might not have to worry about that anymore, though.

"And God..." she halted as her face stung with emotion. Somehow, right now, she knew she needed to call Him another name. Something that recognized Him as her eternal father. "Abba," she finally breathed again. "I need You. I've lost the Hillman account. I have no idea how I'm going to make ends meet. I need You, Daddy," she cried. "You promised that we could cast our cares on you." She couldn't remember the scripture or the exact words, but she remembered the meaning. "So I'm doing that now in Jesus's name. Amen."

Tiffany felt stronger already having spoken the

Word, but she tapped her way to the Bible search app to find the reference. 1 Peter 5:7. She picked up her white leather King James Bible from the coffee table, found the scripture, and read it out loud. *Casting all your care upon him; for he careth for you.* To keep the context, she read the entire chapter, finding even more comfort in verses ten and eleven. *But the God of all grace, who hath called us unto his eternal glory by Christ Jesus, after that ye have suffered a while, make you perfect, stablish, strengthen, settle you. To him be glory and dominion forever and ever. Amen.*

For as much as she wanted to call or text Braxton, Tiffany knew the timing wasn't right. She had seen the defeated expression on his face. He needed to process.

Forget Braxton, *Tiffany* needed some time. Now that Braxton had run off one bird she had in the bush, she didn't have time to make up with him. All her energies had to focus on winning the Red Sea contract. Show time was Monday afternoon at 2 p.m. She had the remainder of Thursday evening plus the weekend to get herself together. Monday morning, she'd drop by the supply store to make copies and arrange presentation folders.

Tiffany set the auto-reply on her email to say that she wouldn't be returning email messages for up to twenty-four hours. She played some Tye Tribbet to pump herself up, ordered a pizza, and settled in for a weekend of working on the biggest presentation of her life. *Here we go, Lord Jesus.*

She shelved the issues with Braxton and her family, diving head-first into a night of reviewing her extensive notes, the teachers' schedules, her maps of the buildings.

Some of the teachers had allowed her to make copies of students' work after they'd blotted out the names. Smiling, Tiffany reviewed several writing samples from third graders.

My favorite food in the world is pizza. The cheese oozes from the slice to your mouth. Yum! I could eat pizza every day, but my mom won't let me because it doesn't have a lot of vegetables. Vegetables should be outlawed!

The students' freedom inspired Tiffany to open her mind to possible ideas for the campus leaders.

They even gave her permission to think freely about her own life. *What if she could, one day, work with kids like these?* Well, maybe not third graders. Too much movement. But she had liked the middle schoolers. Even the oldest kids—with their know-it-all moments—had been a pleasure to observe.

Key word: observe.

Tiffany suspected the students might have been on their best behavior because she was a guest in the room. That had certainly proven true when Braxton took over discipline in that one class.

She waded through more notes and found herself dozing off. Rather than take a shot of her energy drink, she decided to save the notes from the interviews until the next day or maybe even Sunday after church. No matter what, she planned to take a rest Monday after the presentation. Hopefully not too much rest, though. She needed this job to start and the invoices to be paid like yesterday.

Chapter 16

Braxton stared at the picture of Brianna on his phone, her beautiful face shining with joy at her last birthday party. He'd sent Alicia two hundred dollars on top of his usual support check so that his daughter could have a bounce house.

They were already talking about the party for next year—some kind of bus loaded with video games, music, and a dance floor.

"Whatever happened to hot dogs and a piñata in the back yard?" he had kidded Alicia.

"Boo, that's old school," she'd informed him.

He sat back in his executive chair now, flicking through more photos from Brianna's party. He'd been doing this almost nonstop since he left Tiffany's apartment.

His computer screen, which displayed the third chart for his big pitch Monday, dimmed, indicating that he'd been away from work almost fifteen minutes.

Braxton jolted the mouse to keep the screen active. He stared at this phone again. *Is she my daughter?*

The image of Brianna disappeared as his father's name replaced the picture on his phone.

"Hey Dad."

"I'm here."

"Coming."

Braxton rocked himself to a stand and walked to let his father in the house. "'Sup old man?" They hugged.

"The older I get, the older you get," his father joined in the game.

"I like the new porch light you installed outside." His father, always the businessman, surveyed the property quickly as he stepped inside the house.

"Thanks. Want to keep it up for the next tenant."

"That's my boy." His dad popped him on the back. "Moving forward with your life."

They passed through the den, down the main hallway and into Braxton's office, formerly the smallest bedroom of the house. Braxton showed his father his latest concern—the tiles coming loose and signs of a possible leak. Together, they lifted up three squares and knocked on the wood underneath.

"Better get Joe over here before the next storm hits," his father agreed. "Looks like too much for me and you."

"Aww, come on. You not up for the challenge?"

His father declined with a shaking head. Though Braxton saw his father at least twice a week at church, he didn't have nearly as many close-up conversations. He could see now that time was taking a toll on the man. More salt than pepper in his hair, deeper wrinkles.

"Your Momma doesn't want me overexerting myself since I hurt my back playing with your Uncle

Shiloh's bunch the other day."

"You go to the doctor?"

"Naaw. Probably a sprain." His father glanced at the computer. "What you workin' on?"

"The Red Sea Academy proposal."

"Oh yeah? Jeff McDonald?" Braxton's father removed his Kangol cap and sat on the futon, his long legs angling awkwardly in front of him.

"Yes. Monday."

"What are your chances?"

"Fifty-fifty," Braxton admitted.

His father sniffed. "You gonna have to believe in yourself a whole lot more than fifty-fifty if you plan to get the job."

"I do plan to land the gig. This is a tough one, though. And my competition...got in my head." Braxton threw himself into his chair again.

His father's eyes tightened. "What do you mean?"

Braxton would rather be having this conversation with one of his brothers, but right now his dad would have to do. If he didn't get this off his chest, he'd never be able to concentrate on the project.

"My main competition is a woman named Tiffany. She was a good friend of mine at Pinkston. We were getting close right before I pledged Lambda Nu. Then we went our separate ways. And now she's back."

"What's the problem?" his father asked matter-of-factly.

"The problem is I like her. And she likes me. But

we got into an argument. About Brianna."

"What about Brianna?"

"Tiffany was saying that Brianna's mother *got around*." Braxton gave air-quotes. "And I should get a D-N-A test."

His father slapped the side of Braxton's chair with the cap. "Son, I told you that a long time ago."

"I know. I guess I wanted Brianna to be mine so much...if she wasn't, I didn't think I had sufficient reason to stay away from alcohol. Every man needs motivation, you know?"

"The motivation has to be based on the truth," his father corrected, "not wishful thinking."

"Yeah. I know that now."

"Good." His father rose, pushed up his knees, which made loud sounds.

"Old man, you need some milk for all that snap-crackle-poppin'?" Braxton teased.

"Football takes a toll," his father acquiesced. "That Tiffany sounds like a smart girl.

"You ought to bring her by the church some time."

"Maybe after Monday. If she'll talk to me again. And if I win the contract."

"What you mean *if* you win?" His father limped a few steps, then settled into his normal gait as they headed toward the front door again.

"I don't know, Dad. If she beats me...wouldn't be cool."

"Nonsense. If she beats you that just means she's

smarter than you. That's what you want in your corner, son—a smart woman who can talk some sense into you, make you see things in a different light. I believe the Lord's got a lot of work for you to do, even more than working with projects like Red Sea. You gonna need a solid helpmate, not one of them ditzy types you always hangin' with."

"Ditzy, Dad?"

"I didn't stutter. You and Jarvis are gonna get enough of these shallow relationships after while." He let himself out the door. "I'm praying for you to do your best, son. That's all I ask. See you at church Sunday. I'll have Joe come by next week about the floor."

"Yes, sir."

"You might wanna call your brothers and have them listen to your presentation, give you some feedback and ideas."

"I'm one step ahead of you, Dad." All three of Braxton's brothers had agreed to meet with him Sunday at Knox's place after church for a run-through.

"Good. I would join you, but your mother and I have to attend a three o'clock service at Bethel Chapel."

"No worries. We can handle it."

"I know you can. Jeff McDonald's a smart man. He knows good people when he sees them. Call me after the presentation."

"Got it."

Braxton stood on the porch, watching his father fold himself into the antique Ford Mustang he only took for a spin a few times a year. He waved as his dad drove away.

Ditzy?

Tiffany was anything but ditzy. She was real. Maybe too real. Everything about her—except the extensions—was simple, yet overpowering. From her heart-shaped face to her long legs, Tiffany was solid. Not to mention a dry wit to balance his stand-up-comedy-style humor. Every time he earned her smile, he felt as though he'd won a gold medal. She was a prize in and of herself.

If what his father said was true, and so far just about everything Reth Stoneworth had said came to pass, there was a ministry waiting down the road. Braxton had no doubt that people needed to hear the truth of God's love, Christ's sacrifice, and the ever-present help of the Holy Spirit.

Whether he needed to get everything in order first or not was still anybody's guess, but there would come a day when he'd be preaching. Maybe flying here and there, or perhaps volunteering to pray for people at a homeless shelter. Didn't matter to him. Either way, he would need a woman who took her faith seriously. And in Braxton's mind, it didn't get more serious than waiting until marriage to have sex.

You gotta have some kind of conviction to hold out this long.

Braxton slowly walked back to his office. Stared

at the computer again. He couldn't work, not with so much on his mind. But he *had* to work. No matter what happened with Brianna, winning Red Sea meant a step-up in his game.

But the matter with Tiff was settled. He needed her. Probably always had. She'd probably been sent by God as a voice of reason in his life, but he'd ignored her when he thought he'd found treasure in the Greek brotherhood.

He could only thank God that no other man had swooped her up. It was as though God had hidden her in a pile of her own professional work, just for him.

He never wanted to lose this treasure again.

Chapter 17

Tiffany hit snooze three times, which meant she'd be sitting in the balcony at church during the last Sunday service. Thankfully, Cassie had been able to save her a spot in the we-too-late-to-be-picky section. She joined her friend as the choir sang its last song, *We Fall Down, But We Get Up*.

Amazed at how God could match her arrival with the perfect entrance song, Tiffany stood and raised her hands in praise. *God, you're right on time even when I'm late.* His faithfulness never ceased to humble her. Despite the vastness of the sanctuary, Tiffany felt as though she was worshipping in a tent with the Lord right by her side.

When Pastor Niles preached a message entitled "Listen and Hear," Tiffany thought she might have to do an old school move and throw a handkerchief at the pulpit 'cause he was (as her grandmother would say) sho' nuff preachin' up her alley!

"I remember, as a child, I was fascinated by the story of Jonah and the whale," Pastor recalled. "And as a teenager, I couldn't understand why Jonah wouldn't want the people of Ninevah saved. Why would anyone want to withhold the goodness of God, when we're so indebted ourselves? Oh, but when I became a young man. After a few people had hurt me."

"Yes!" the congregation roared.

"After I'd trusted one too many times."

People stood and clapped.

"Oh, then I understood Jonah. See, once you see people for who they are, their true colors, it's really easy to forget our own problems. Our own issues. The people *we've* hurt."

Waves of agreement swept through the crowd.

"The ones *we* shut out. Rejected. Failed to take an extra step to reach."

Tiffany whispered, "Lord, search my heart."

Braxton's face came to mind. Not today's Braxton—old Braxton. Neophyte Lambda Nu Braxton. She remembered the day after he pledged. He came to her dorm room. Half-drunk. With the letter "L" branded on his upper right arm.

She remembered the smell of his burned flesh and how it almost made her vomit. "That's gross!" She had exclaimed.

"Fi-yah!"

Disgusted, she had mouthed off, "Do you have any idea of the history behind branding people? How our people were brutalized? Didn't you watch *Roots* in, like, the eighth grade?"

"Tiff, this is *Lambda Nu,* baby!"

She knew he was too far gone to process her reason. Plus the alcohol. So she'd left him standing in the lobby and gone to breakfast by herself wondering what he might do next.

She realized now, as Pastor Niles talked about

Jonah's resentment, that instead of helping Braxton stay grounded, she'd left him to himself.

But Braxton wasn't my responsibility, Lord.

Yet, as quickly as she'd refuted, the answer came in her heart: *But it is your responsibility to remain who I am in You.*

As she blinked back tears, Tiffany recalled how quickly she'd cut Braxton out of her life. Not that she was meant to marry the man at age twenty. Yet, she made the decision from pain, not even once asking God for an opinion.

Yeah, I've got a bad habit of that, Father. Forgive me.

As the sermon continued, Tiffany felt her heart warming to the idea that she and Braxton needed one another. Always had. He'd become her best friend their freshman year—two young adults away from home, trying to find their way. Just happened to have similar church backgrounds, be put together on their first project, and were somehow kept from a physical attraction toward one another until the time was right.

Like now.

She remembered how perfect His timing had been, even on this morning.

He's never late—even when I am.

Following the benediction, Cassie talked Tiffany into a quick brunch at a small café a few blocks from the church. "Girl, when you do get the bid, I probably won't see you for a year."

"True that," Tiffany agreed with a slight chuckle.

They seated themselves in a booth by the fireplace and ordered soups and sandwiches. Just enough to stave off hunger, but not enough to make Tiffany too sleepy to work.

Cassie jumped to the topic of Braxton right away. "So, what's up with you and the preacher's kid?"

Cornered but happy to actually talk to someone about him, Tiffany shared, "Girl. We had this blow-up two nights ago. I was going on and on about this girl in our college yearbook. Turns out, the girl was his daughter's mother."

"Ooh, snap."

"Snap is right. He was so ready to leave."

"But this is a good thing," Cassie said, holding up her index finger. "You've seen him mad."

"How is mad good?"

"My mom always said you need to see people at their worst to know if you can deal with their kind of crazy," she said. "Sounds like he's a let-me-walk-away-and-think type. Not bad. I've seen worse."

"You're the queen of optimism."

"I know," she cheesed. "So now what?"

"Here comes part B," Tiffany continued. "So I'm sitting there trying to take back my words when I get a call from my *now-former* contractor saying that they'd told me about a meeting, but I never got the message. When I get off the phone with them, Braxton's like 'oh, I'm sorry, Tiff. When we were riding back from your mom's, you went to sleep so I sent it to voice mail.' And I'm like what?!"

Cassie waved. "Wait back up. You took him to meet your mom already? You gotta catch me up."

"It wasn't like that. I didn't have the cash-a-roni to pay my mom's gardener. She was all in a tizzy, so I asked Braxton to come take care of it."

In awe, Cassie asked, "This man done came over to your momma's house and mowed her grass for her?"

"Yes."

Wide-eyed, Cassie asked in a dopey tone, "And what the problem is?"

"The problem is he caused me to lose a job! He—"

Cassie's hand became a stop sign. "Please! First things first. Any man who will tend to your momma's lawn deserves a medal. Secondly, he probably turned off your phone after he saw the dark circles under your eyes and decided to protect you from your workaholic self!"

"Umm...are you my friend or Braxton's friend?"

"I'm *right's* friend. And for the record, if you were passed out in the car, looking as tired as you looked when you came over my house the other night, I would have done the same thing, *my* friend."

"Did I look that bad?" Tiffany fretted. She picked up the chrome napkin holder and stared at her reflection.

Cassie added, "Burr-roke. Down. Girl, we talked about you real bad when you left. Thought about calling one of your sisters." Cassie poked out her lips, shaking her head.

Tiffany rolled her eyes, returned the napkin holder to its place, then resigned with a sigh. "I don't know what I'm gonna do if I get this client, Cassie. It's *way* more work than I've ever taken on. Huge learning curve."

"But you're down a client, right?"

"Yes. I do have more time in my schedule. And I really want to work at Red Sea. I'd be around kids. The high school kids were amazing." Tiffany perked up as she recounted her visits with the older students.

Cassie listened, asking questions and interjecting insights, some of which Tiffany even thought were noteworthy for the presentation. She pressed her phone into action. "Let me write that down."

When her screen illuminated, she saw the notification of an email from Rhonda. "I'm sorry. I need to read this email. It's from Red Sea."

"Go ahead. I'm gonna refill my tea."

Cassie journeyed to the beverage bar while Tiffany read the message.

Miss Warren, please be advised that your presentation time has been moved to 9:00 am. Miss Deja Robinson experienced a family emergency and needs to present her proposal later in the day. Please let us know that you received this message and whether the switch will work for you. If not, we can reschedule, but I must advise you that Mr. McDonald has no other time slots available until Thursday afternoon.

Thank you!

No! No! No! Tomorrow morning was no good, and she wasn't willing to drag this out until Thursday, not when there was a possibility she might need to be looking for other work in the meantime.

Tiffany got the irresistible urge to check Deja's Facebook page and find out what type of family emergency was happening in this chick's life. If her former co-worker was the FB-addict she had always been, Deja would have already posted way too much information.

Deja's latest post, however, showed Deja's current situation—posted three minutes earlier—was "turnt- up" at the bar with three friends drinking martinis, according to her description.

No she didn't!

Yes she did.

"Ooh!" Tiffany grumbled to herself. "Should have known." The old hit-'em-last was one of the tricky strategies they'd been taught to master at Langley. Based on industry research, they were told to manipulate what they could to place themselves in a position to share their presentations last—to leave an impression in potential clients' minds.

Obviously, Deja had successfully played that trick with folks at Red Sea.

If Tiffany had been a bad sport, she'd have taken a screen shot and sent it back to Mr. McDonald's secretary with a caption: *What kind of family emergency is THIS?*

She couldn't do that without making herself look bad, though. Tiffany simply hit reply and typed: No problem. See you all in the morning.

Backed into a corner now, Tiffany's work-brain kicked into gear as she re-worked the logistics. It was Sunday, so the office supply store would close at 6:00 p.m. She wouldn't be finished with the files before 6:00. That wouldn't work.

Maybe she could get up early and make the copies in the morning. *Hmmm*...the store didn't open until 8:00 a.m. *Nope.* Even if she were standing at the doors when they opened, she wouldn't have enough time to make the copies, punch holes, assemble the folders and get to Red Sea before 9:00. She could do black-and-white copies...if she had enough toner. *Do I have enough toner?* Even if she did have enough toner, the monochrome print wouldn't be nearly as attractive as Deja's or Braxton's.

She could hit up the twenty-four hour Kinkos in downtown Dallas. Or maybe the one in Arlington, that stayed open until 9pm. Copies would cost a lot more. Not to mention gas. She didn't have that kind of money to spare.

Plus she'd be pooped in the morning. *I'm gonna need an energy drink.*

The waiter brought their orders to the table. "Tomato bisque?"

"Yes, that's mine. And I'm so sorry, but I'm going to have to ask you to make it to-go. I have to leave."

"No problem. Should I make your friend's to go as well?"

"She'll probably stay."

The waitress slid Cassie's food onto the table.

"Be right back."

"Thank you."

Cassie returned. "Was there something wrong with your food?"

"No. I gotta go. My presentation is tomorrow morning instead of tomorrow afternoon. I still need to proof the slides, make copies. Ugh!"

"Is there anything I can do to help?"

Tiffany's auto-pilot declared, "No. I got this."

"Wait." Cassie put a hand on Tiffany's arm. "You didn't even consider my question before you answered. So let me ask again. Is there anything I can do to help?"

Tiffany closed her eyes and wished. "You got a color printer?"

"As a matter of fact, I do."

Tiffany's eyes popped open in delight.

"High-quality. Just replaced the ink cartridges. High-yield," Cassie said.

"May I borrow it? I'll replace the ink when I get paid at the end of the month."

"Of course. See? Problem solved. Girl, I know it's hard, but we gotta learn how to accept help. Superwoman is wack."

When their server brought Tiffany's food in its to-go container, Tiffany didn't have the heart to tell her she was going to eat it at the restaurant after all. One more trip back to the kitchen might not have gone over well with the chef.

Once the lady was out of view, Tiffany opened the container and enjoyed a relaxing lunch. The very idea of admitting to herself that she—the one-woman-show—needed help was refreshing. Freed her to spend time with one of her best friends on a beautiful Sunday afternoon.

No energy drink needed.

"So when are you going to call him back?" Cassie asked.

"Why would I call him back?"

"Sounds to me like you're the one who kicked him out."

"Yeah," Tiffany agreed, "but he was about to leave. Anyway, if I call him back, that would give him the upper hand, right? I mean, I'm not desperate here. I *can* get a man."

"A good one like Braxton?"

"I don't know." Tiffany laughed at herself. "I'm just saying. If I make the first move toward reconciliation, that makes me the weak one."

Cassie tapped her glass with a fork. "Listen up. Are you hearing the words that are coming out of your mouth?"

"Yes!"

"Did you hear the words coming out of Pastor Niles's mouth, what, thirty minutes ago?"

"Yessss." Tiffany tried to connect the dots between the sermon and Cassie's forthcoming lecture.

Cassie must have thought she was taking too long to understand. "Jonah was playing games, worrying about people taking advantage of God's love. You can't live your life worrying about what the score is. You certainly can't fall in love worrying about who's gonna have the so-called upper-hand. We're almost thirty. We gotta stop with the kid's stuff. Walk in Christ's love. If you mess up, apologize. You be you. Period."

Cassie's words confirmed those of their Father. That was all Tiffany needed to hear.

They finished lunch. Tiffany followed Cassie to get the printer. Afterward, she stopped by the office supply store and purchased the materials needed. Knowing that she had gained back some of her time by literally printing in-house, she could relax a little more. Get into the groove.

This help thing is pretty good.

Somewhere between the paper aisle and the folder aisle, thoughts of Braxton invaded her mind again. She wondered if he was working on his presentation. *Did he go to church today? Who did he eat lunch with? Is he still mad at me? Wait—was he ever mad at me to begin with?*

Tiffany resolved to send him a text.

Hope things go well for you tomorrow. May the best project manager win.

Seconds later, he replied with the words:

Quotation mark.

She giggled at his replacement for the word ditto. She sent him a smiley face.

He sent her a thumbs-up.

Tiffany wished she'd called him instead. These emoticons weren't telling her how he felt.

Or maybe they were. Maybe he'd had enough of her resistance. But what was she supposed to do—just admit to him that she was falling for him again? Throw herself at his Lambda Nu boots like all the other women?

This was why she didn't do relationships. She didn't have the time nor the aptitude for these games. Braxton would have to take her as she was—even if it meant he might hurt her again.

But at least this time she'd know she'd given their relationship a fighting chance.

Chapter 18

Braxton identified himself to building security and was allowed to proceed toward the elevator. Upon entering the elevator, he pressed the code to access Knox's floor in the swanky downtown Dallas high-rise, a testament to his desire to be left alone. What Knox called serious Braxton called hermit-ish. It wasn't until he was in the familiar, safe company of his three brothers that the Knox Stoneworth they'd grown up with stepped forward.

This new guy in his brother's body had been birthed a few years ago after Knox's fiancé dumped him at the altar. Literally. Like one of those chick flicks where the girl realizes at the last minute that she doesn't love the nice, stable guy she's about to marry. She's still madly in love with her ex who decides to "speak now" instead of forever holding his peace.

Those kinds of scenes make people cheer for the woman and her true love, but what about the guy left standing at the altar? He moves into an exclusive building, buries himself in work, and turns down every invitation to a double-date offered.

Braxton exited the elevator and walked to the end of the hallway. He rang the doorbell, then heard the door lock from within.

Standing an inch taller than Braxton was his older

brother, Knox, holding a chicken wing in one hand and a coke in the other. Even as adults, Braxton appreciated still being able to look up to his brother, literally.

"'Sup?"

"Nothing much," Braxton said.

They hugged to the extent possible with Knox's full hands and Braxton's weighted down by his computer and binder.

Jarvis and West acknowledged Braxton only half-heartedly. They were headlong into a game of Madden, which gave Braxton some time to have a snack and catch up with Knox.

"Want some wings?"

"What flavors you got?" Braxton asked, straddling a stool to sit. He placed his elbows on the cool granite countertop. The contemporary kitchen actually reminded him of Tiffany's, spotless to the point of being almost empty.

"Traditional, atomic, lemon pepper."

"Where'd you get 'em?"

Knox stopped short of grabbing a paper plate from the plastic sheath. "You hungry or not? Asking all these questions."

Braxton had to laugh at himself, "Aiiight, aiiiight. Lemon pepper."

"Thank you," Knox laughed. "Coming in here like this is Burger King, tryna have it your way."

It was nice to hear his brother chide him. Braxton wished that someone or something would happen to get Knox back to himself again one hundred percent of the time.

Knox presented Braxton with six wings, a tall glass of tea, and a napkin.

"Thanks, bro."

"No problem. How long's the presentation?"

"Thirty, forty minutes."

"We'd better get started soon. I'm going to work at seven."

"On a Sunday?" Braxton questioned. "Those dogs and cats aren't going anywhere, you know."

"Cowboys play San Diego tonight," Jarvis noted.

"Sunday is when I can get the most work done," Knox said.

"Whooo!" Jarvis hollered in victory. "That's what I'm talkin' about!"

"Ridiculous!" West protested. "My receivers are bootleg!"

"Whooo!" from Jarvis again.

Those two could get seriously competitive and highly offended in a heartbeat.

"Let's go ahead and start on Braxton's thing," Knox assumed his big brother role easily.

West whined, "Man, I gotta use the restroom."

"You probably do after that beatin' I put on you," Jarvis teased, rocking back into the brown suede sofa in laughter.

Once the men were all assembled on Knox's furniture and Braxton hooked up his presentation station to Knox's fifty-inch television, the business began. For the next ninety minutes, Braxton ran through his presentation, listened to feedback, and answered questions that helped him sharpen his plan for the next day.

Jarvis's comments pertained mostly to layout and physical presentation on the screen. He even caught a few spelling errors. West critiqued the timing, prompting Braxton to reorder slides to streamline his ideas. Knox, of course, asked the kinds of probing questions that helped Braxton refine the concepts in his own brain. Together, the brothers tightened Braxton's production such that if Braxton had to give his presentation a grade before and after their run-through, he would have gone from a B- to an A+.

"Yo, thanks. I'mma kill it tomorrow!" Braxton said. He saved the changes and powered down the laptop.

"That's how we do it," Knox said.

West's phone rang. "Hey. This is Rainey. I'll put her on speaker." He pressed the microphone button and set the device on Knox's coffee table. The four brothers gathered closely.

Somehow, each man's voice seemed to elevate half an octave as they greeted their baby sister, one by one. Though she was twenty-three years old and nearly a Ph.D., she was still "baby Rainey" to them. Always would be.

"Hi guys," she sang through the phone, "I miss you all."

"We know you won't be home for Christmas

because of the mini-mester. But you're coming home for Mom and Dad's thirty-fifth anniversary party in February, right?" Jarvis asked.

"Yes, thanks to Knox."

"Anything you need," he said. "We're all proud of you."

"Actually, that's what I'm calling about," Rainey sing-songed. "Um…West, can you take me off speakerphone, please?"

It was no secret that, being closest in age to Rainey, West shared a special relationship with his sister. But the other brothers weren't having it.

"What's up?" Braxton asked.

"Yeah. If it's about Mom and Dad, we'd like to hear, too," Jarvis pressed.

Rainey sighed. "Okay. I might as well get it over with."

All four brothers took turns looking at each other, faces hardening, silently wondering what might be wrong with their little sister.

"What's up?" Knox asked.

"I *am* coming to the anniversary. And I'm bringing someone with me."

"What?!" from Jarvis.

"Who is it?" Knox demanded.

"Is this a *boyfriend*?" from Braxton.

"Send us a picture," West ordered. "And a full name and social security number"

"Stop it! All of you! See, this is why I didn't even want to tell you people. Yes, he is my boyfriend.

We're very serious about one another."

Braxton tried to fathom this mystery. *Rainey has a boyfriend? A serious boyfriend.* He wasn't even sure his sister was allowed to have boyfriends yet.

"What did Dad say?" Jarvis asked.

"I haven't told him yet. That's why I was calling to talk to *West.* I wanted him to, you know, soften Daddy up for me because when I come home, Elvin and I…"

"Elvin?" the brothers exclaimed.

"What kind of name is that?" Jarvis asked. "He related to El-*vis*?"

"Stop overreacting. I'm twenty-three years old. I'm not a baby anymore, Stoneworth men. It's time to let me grow up."

It didn't take much longer for Rainey to realize that she wasn't going to get any help from this group.

"West, I'll call you later. I love you all. Talk to you later."

"I'mma call *you* later," Jarvis threatened.

"Maybe tomorrow, Jarvis. *Not* tonight," Rainey told him.

"Why? What you doin' tonight?" Jarvis challenged.

"Bye."

The phone screen went black.

"Man, I ain't ready for this." Knox shook his head.

"I hear you," Braxton echoed.

They talked for a while longer about the horrific

idea of their sister falling in love. Dating. Bringing someone home to meet the family. Up until now, Rainey had been so busy passing tests and earning 4.0 GPAs and numerous scholarships, she hadn't had time to have a boyfriend. She'd barely had a prom date.

"We need to pray," West said. "For Braxton's presentation, of course. For Rainey. And for all of us 'cause I'm telling you—if somebody messes over my sister, we gon' have ourselves a serious problem."

"Amen and it is so," Jarvis agreed.

Knox sighed. "Well, she can't be a baby forever. I guess."

"Whatever," Jarvis huffed.

"Twenty-three isn't exactly twelve." Braxton laughed. Knox and West followed suit.

"I ain't playin'," Jarvis said. "If I see any kind of shadow of shade, I'm all over *Eyul-vin*."

Knox laughed. "Yeah, let's pray."

Chapter 19

Tiffany stayed up until 1:30 a.m. pulling her final thoughts together and getting them on smooth, heavyweight paper in colored ink. She thanked God for Cassie. For the printer. For ink. By that time, she was also thankful for a pillow and a blanket.

With only five hours of sleep, her first inclination was to grab the bottle of energy in her refrigerator. But somehow Braxton—whom she hadn't spoken to in almost three days—seemed to still be in her head, warning her against its effects.

She needed something to jumpstart her brain, still a bit frazzled by a long evening of work as well as some anxiety about this morning. Deja's stunt had put a major kink in Tiffany's plan.

That girl need Jesus, she thought.

And then it occurred to Tiffany that *she* needed Jesus, too. *Pastor's boomerang Jonah message is working a little too well.*

Nonetheless, Tiffany opened her Bible to the concordance and found scriptures to address fear. She settled on Philippians 4, reading the chapter in its entirety. She began to speak to the Lord about her cares, her fears. The more she spoke, the more issues bubbled to the surface in prayer.

"God, about my daddy. I know he's with You, so I'm not worried about him. I miss him, You know I do. But You promised to never leave me, nor forsake me. Be with me today when I present. And be with Braxton, too. And I guess Deja, too, if she's Yours. I give this Red Sea project to you. If it's for me, it will work out. If it's not, I pray that You will award it to whoever is the best fit. I trust Your judgment, God. Amen."

And with that, Tiffany surrendered her plans to God. If this contract was hers, the presentation would go well. They would pick her, and then God would grace her to do the job well.

If not...well, everybody goes through hard times. God would have to pull her through.

Braxton's foot tapped impatiently on the tiled floor. This would be over in an hour or so, he hoped. What was done would be done, and he could resume with the plans he had for both Brianna and Tiffany.

Yesterday, he had called Alicia and asked for a DNA test.

"Why do you want one now?" Alicia had asked in a surprisingly calm voice.

"I want to settle the issue of paternity legally, so there will never be a question in anyone's mind."

"The only mind questioning it is yours."

He waited to make sure she didn't have anything else to add—cutting Alicia off was never a good idea.

"I have to confess that I've been using Brianna as my motivation. When you told me that I was a father, that news came at a time when I really needed a reason to push. So I didn't allow myself to respond to the questions in my mind. But I really think it's important that my motivations be based on the truth," he repeated his father's words almost verbatim.

"What makes you think you're not her father?" Alicia fired.

"I just want to be sure," Braxton admitted. "I mean...those were some wild days, back at Pinkston. Have you...ever wondered?"

Alicia answered a little too quickly, "She looks like you."

"You're not answering my question."

"Braxton, that was all a long time ago. We were all living like hippies—free love, no restraints, do what feels good. Just so happens, a woman can only give birth once every nine months. But for all we know, you might have three or four kids."

Alicia had given thought to his worst nightmare—more kids coming out of the woodwork.

"I gotta take it one child at a time," he admitted. "I can fly up that way in January, after the holidays, when fares go down."

"Fine. And if she's yours—which I'm pretty sure she is—we're going through the courts for child support."

"Okay."

The pressure of becoming a father on record weighed heavily on him this morning, causing Braxton to open his notes once again on the iPad.

Today meant everything.

The door to the executive offices opened, and out walked Tiffany in a gray suit, her long strides testifying to years of athletic training, her face set in confidence and her hair swaying with each step.

He stood, fighting the urge to hug her. "How'd it go?"

"Pretty good. Lots of questions. Be prepared."

"Thank you," he said with a nod.

They stood face-to-face for an awkward second.

"Bra—"

"Ti—"

They both stopped in the middle of each other's names, simultaneously. Laughed.

"Ladies first."

Tiffany breathed deeply. "Braxton, I want to apologize. I shouldn't have spoken badly about Alicia."

"And I apologize for not letting you know you'd missed a call. It really did slip my mind."

Rhonda interrupted from behind the receptionist's counter. "Mr. Stoneworth, Mr. McDonald and the committee will see you know."

Braxton straightened his tie. "Thank you, Rhonda."

"Break a leg," Tiffany said, running her hand along his lapel.

Braxton closed in the space between them and whispered, "Look. I don't care what happens with this contract. Whether I get it or not, I still want you."

Tiffany's face brightened. "I was thinking the same thing."

"Will you wait for me?" he asked.

"Wait?"

"Yeah. Right here. We can do brunch after. Compare notes, finally."

"I've been waiting for you for a long time," Tiffany admitted with tears in her eyes. "What's another half-hour or so?"

He kissed her cheek. "You won't be sorry."

Pumped by the thought of meeting Tiffany afterward. The committee, which consisted of Mr. McDonald, six teachers—two from elementary, middle, and high school—and old boy from the physical education classes, whom Braxton had seen sniffing around Deja. Thank God she'd found someone else to harass.

Braxton breezed through his presentation. He outlined the strengths and weakness of their communication systems, classified the team leaders' styles, and presented a plan to train and support the leaders they had in place so that each teacher would have an accountability partner and a means to measure success beyond student achievement on multiple choice assessments.

If there was ever a time he felt "Help" coming on, it was during the question-and-answer phase, which felt more like a cross-examination than a professional probing. And the person with the most grilling inquiry was the PE man, who actually had the least changes up ahead. It only took a minute for Braxton to see that the guy was trying to cast doubt on Braxton's competence. He was paving the way for Deja to blow the group away.

But, thanks to Knox's sharp inquiry, Braxton was ready for this dude's questions and then some.

Braxton left the meeting feeling like Rocky in his first movie after the last fight—without the swollen eyes. But his "Adrian," Tiffany, would be waiting for him when this was all over. Win, lose, or draw—he had already won.

With Rhonda's permission, Tiffany waited in the reception area rather than going to her car to either freeze or waste gas while waiting for Braxton.

It was a shame her budget had come down to simple things like gas money. "Lord, I need a breakthrough."

"Can I get you some coffee?" Rhonda asked after about ten minutes of waiting.

"No, thanks. I'm not really a coffee girl."

"Coffee is sacred around here," Rhonda joked.

"Yes. People feel almost entitled to it."

Rhonda wiggled her torso a bit and leaned over the counter. "I see you and Mr. Stoneworth have become acquainted."

"Oh, we've known each other since college. He's an old friend."

"He's quite fond of you," Rhonda observed in a

lowered tone.

Tiffany hid a smile. "I guess."

"Well, I know you both can't win the contract. But maybe this wasn't about the contract, you know? All things work out for the good of those who love the Lord."

"Amen," Rhonda agreed as Tiffany considered, for the first time, that maybe God had orchestrated this entire deal for reasons all His own.

When Braxton emerged through the doorway about an hour later, Tiffany could have read his "I'm-the-man" expression from ten miles away. "Must have gone well."

"Girl, if we weren't in the school lobby, I'd pick you up and swing you around."

"Don't stop on my account!" Rhonda boomed.

Braxton released the handle of his computer bag and dropped his iPad on a chair. Before Tiffany could stop him, he grabbed her by the waist and twirled her in the air.

She held on for dear life. "Braxton! Put me down!"

He went around another 360 degrees, then allowed her feet to touch the floor again. "Man, that felt good."

Tiffany, breathless from his touch, pressed her clothes back in place. "I'm glad the meeting was so exhilarating."

"I wasn't talking about the meeting. *You* felt good in my arms."

Rhonda folded her hands like she was watching a Hallmark movie. "Awwwww."

Tiffany felt her face growing warm. "Shall we do brunch now?"

"Absolutely."

Braxton tucked his tablet in the rolling computer bag, freeing his right hand to hold Tiffany's left.

Unwilling to be separated from her, Braxton insisted they ride together. "We won't go far."

"So long as we skirt around the half-day kindergarten traffic," Tiffany added a condition.

"Got it."

Eating a light lunch didn't seem fitting for the occasion. If he was going to share his whole heart with Tiffany, he'd much prefer something heavy— barbecue or Italian.

Come to think of it, he was too nervous to eat. He started the car. "You starving?"

"No."

"You wanna do something a little different for lunch?"

"Depends."

"You trust me?" he asked her.

Tiffany's jaw tightened for a second, but a grin loosened the tension. "Yes."

Braxton kissed her full lips. "Let's go."

Chapter 20

Braxton stopped the car in an old downtown Dallas shopping center with a parade of several unique-sounding stores. Larry's Locker boasted personalized footwear. There was also a gourmet popcorn shop and some French place Tiffany couldn't pronounce.

When he opened her car door, Tiffany finally asked, "Where are we going?"

"We're going to my mom's favorite place in the whole wide world."

"What?"

"I have to come here every year to get her something for Christmas. It's cool in a weird way." He took Tiffany's hand and led her into the French place. As they neared the entrance, Tiffany could see that this venue was packed with kitchenware.

"Is this the Martha Stewart store?"

"Might as well be."

They walked through the entrance. The shining utensils and dishware—some hanging from the ceiling—took Tiffany by surprise. She probably would have liked it, if she'd been into cooking. "Ummm…I can see why this is your mom's favorite store, but why'd you bring me here?"

"Bonjour, Braxton! How are you?" A short woman dressed in exactly what Tiffany thought a

French chef would wear came from behind and hugged Braxton.

"Bonjour, Claire. This is my friend, Tiffany."

"Oh! She is quite lovely!" The woman shook Tiffany's hand.

"Thank you."

"And your mother? Will she come to class today?"

"No. I didn't have time to swing by and get her. I brought Tiffany instead."

Class? She squeezed Braxton's arm.

"What are we having?" he asked Claire.

"Oh! You love it, Braxton. Italian spinach and kale pizza. To die for." Claire gathered her fingertips and touched them to her lips. "We shall start in ten minutes. Get your aprons?"

"Yes." Braxton said.

"A cooking class?" Tiffany asked.

"Yep." He paid their fee at the register while Tiffany watched in disbelief.

"You know I have no kitchen skills, right?"

"Yeah, but remember what I told you. The woman I'm with has to know how to burn in the kitchen."

"And I told you—good for *her*."

Braxton broke Tiffany's resolve with another kiss. "It's okay, baby. Even if I do all the cooking, I still want you by my side. You can just stand there. Reading the recipe. Giving me the ingredients."

Tiffany laughed. "Are you serious?"

"More than I've ever been."

Braxton's chestnut eyes locked onto hers as an intense peace washed over Tiffany. This was exactly where she belonged right this very moment. She'd never been more sure of anything in her life. *Thank You, Lord.*

The cooking partnerships were stationed at large steel tables. Under Claire's careful guidance, Tiffany sautéed the garlic, onions, and bacon bits in butter. Braxton cooked the Italian sausage. Together, they washed and prepared the kale, lightly salting and then spritzing with fresh lemon juice.

Tiffany shared with Braxton, "I don't know about putting kale on a pizza."

"You'd better not let Miss Claire hear you doubting her recipe."

"She's French. Pizza is Italian."

"Are you trying to get us kicked out of here?"

"No. I'm just saying," Tiffany argued, "we should be able to modify the recipe."

Braxton blinked slowly. "If you—a woman who has already told me she cannot cook—would like to change the recipe given to us by, like, a black belt chef…"

"There's no such thing," Tiffany snickered, her head still down as she sliced the Mozarella cheese. Though the class had ten members, Tiffany and Braxton were in their own little world.

Braxton ventured to ask Miss Claire if they could add other spices to their creation.

"You have every right to ruin your pizza if you'd

like."

Braxton bowed. "Thank you."

He and Tiffany spent several minutes smelling the spices, hoping for the perfect mix of flavor and heat.

Miss Claire whispered to them as Braxton lifted the pizza into the oven. "I expect yours to taste the best, since you two have prepared it with such amour."

"Awwww." Tiffany sounded like she was the one watching romance movies now.

"Ar-*more*?" Braxton fussed. "I didn't put no Arm-n-Hammer in there!"

Tiffany slapped his arm.

"Amour!" Claire said again. "Love! Love, I tell you!"

"I know, Miss Claire. I'm just messing with you."

"My word," the woman tsked "You are always pulling my leg, Braxton."

"Don't bother, Miss Claire. He pulls mine, too."

"Yes, but I am sure you like it," the woman teased Tiffany.

"Oooop!" Tiffany exclaimed.

"Watch out now, Miss Claire," Braxton said, wagging his finger.

The woman waved him off. "I am only kidding with you two love-birds. Be sure to clean up your area, Braxton. You have dropped many pieces. A messy cook you are." She pointed at Tiffany's side of the table. "The lady, however, is very clean."

"Thank you, Miss Claire," Tiffany gloated as their

instructor walked away.

Braxton flicked leftover bits of dough at Tiffany.

"I know you didn't!" She made sure Miss Claire wasn't looking, then flicked some back at him.

"Stop before you get us in trouble."

"You started it."

Miss Claire turned and accosted them. "Is there a problem?"

"No," Braxton and Tiffany said in unison.

Braxton poked Tiffany's waist.

"Ow!"

Miss Claire shook her head. "You two." She gave her attention to another table.

They could hardly clean up for flirting, giving Tiffany an excuse to keep her smile front and center. No need to hide it or keep Braxton from seeing her true feelings anymore. She was finally free to love.

Tiffany's phone vibrated in her pocket. She stepped away from the table, wiped her hands on the apron and answered. "Hello?"

"Tiffany, I need you to come over here right now! Mr. Lewis's dog dug a hole under the fence! Went in my backyard and scratched up all my patio furniture cushions!"

Not willing to add to the drama, Tiffany asked, "Momma, have you called Mr. Lewis?"

"No! I'm calling you first so you can deal with it—you know the Lewis's always been kinda crazy. Your daddy used to handle them."

"I'm sorry. I can't. I've got enough pressure on

me right now from work. It's time you started dealing with some things yourself," Tiffany tried to encourage her.

Her mother fussed, "So you just gonna leave me to fend for myself?"

"Momma, I know Daddy used to handle everything when he was alive. But he's gone now. Things have to change. You're perfectly capable of having a conversation with neighbors and reaching a solution. Ask the Lord to give you the right words. He will do it."

Silence.

"Did you hear me?"

"Yes."

"Okay, well…I gotta go."

Tiffany already knew what her mother would do next: Call her sisters and tell on Tiffany. Hopefully, Terri Anne would take up for Tiffany. But if she didn't, they'd all have to work through all this later. Tiffany wasn't about to let news of a dog's mischief ruin her day with Braxton.

When Miss Claire cut their pizza and presented it to them fresh out of the hearth stove, Tiffany and Braxton "toasted" with their slices.

"To us," Braxton declared.

"To us."

Pizza had never tasted so good.

Braxton and Tiffany returned to the Red Sea

Academy's visitor's parking shortly after 1pm.

"That was fun," she complimented him.

"I'm glad you enjoyed it. Want to do it again?"

"On a Saturday, 'cause one of us is about to have all our weekdays filled to capacity," Tiffany said. "From the way you looked when you left your meeting, I'm a tad bit scared."

He gave her a semi-sympathetic glance. "I nailed it, Tiff."

She rolled her eyes. "Guess we'll find out tomorrow, huh?"

"Guess so. I've got another big reveal coming up soon," Braxton offered. "Brianna's paternity test."

Tiffany hesitated. "You're going to have it done?"

"Yeah. Alicia agreed. Sounds like maybe she wants closure on the matter, too."

"Makes sense."

Braxton drummed on the steering wheel. "What if she's not mine? What if the guy who is her biological father doesn't step up to the plate?"

"There's no rule saying you have to leave her life," Tiffany said. "Maybe you could be her godfather? I mean, you and Alicia seem pretty civil."

Braxton pinched his upper lip. "I don't know. I don't want to confuse her even more."

"Let's just wait and see."

He liked the way Tiffany said "let's," like she was in it with him. "Yeah. Nothing else to do but wait."

A car pulled in the empty space on Braxton's side. He turned his head slightly to check out their surroundings. He recognized the car as Deja's. There was a man seated beside her.

Tiffany asked, "Isn't that the guy from the committee?"

Braxton looked again. Same brown suit with white jacket. He and Deja were involved in quite an animated conversation, with arm motions and emphasizing imaginary points in the air. Didn't take long for Braxton to assess the situation. "This dude's telling her everything we said in our presentations."

Tiffany reached over Braxton's arm and blew the horn.

Deja and PE man's heads whipped around.

"Lying cheater!" Tiffany yelled in rather close proximity to Braxton's ear.

"Tiff, they can't hear you. Although *I* can."

"Don't you see? She is such a snake! She switched times with me so that she could leave a lasting impression, she sweet-talked this mole to get information to shoot down our points and enhance her presentation," Tiffany surmised.

"Shade," Braxton murmured.

Deja and the man quickly got out of her car. She walked to the front of the administration building. He entered through one of the side doors.

"Ridiculous. If she gets this account—"

"She won't," Braxton said calmly. "If she does, it'll blow up in her face and they'll have to call one of us back."

Tiffany sat back. "How can you be sure?"

"Look around."

His hand swept across the view of the magnificent buildings and landscaping Tiffany had been impressed with from the moment she stepped on campus. "This place is anointed," Braxton spoke, "and Mr. McDonald is a man of God. Evil won't prosper here. The only way she'd be able to stay is if she changes. Who knows? God might use this place to change *her*."

Tiffany's narrowed gaze burned on Deja's car.

"I can see you're getting unreasonably crunk about this situation. You wanna pray?"

"I don't know what we're praying for, but go."

Braxton laced his hand with hers. "Father, thank You for Your son, Christ. In Him we have life, love, and hope. We thank You for the assurance in Your word that no weapon formed against us prospers. We speak Your perfect will into this situation. You know exactly what's happening and we thank You in advance for watching over Your word to make sure that it is performed. Be glorified in this outcome. In Jesus's name, Amen."

"Amen."

Tiffany breathed easy again. "You remind me of my best friend. So optimistic."

"I want to be your best friend again."

Tiffany cupped Braxton's warm face and planted two soft kisses on his cheek. "You always know exactly what to say."

His gave her a Kool-Aid grin. "I try."

"No. I don't think you're trying, Braxton. It's you. You know how to make me laugh, when to get serious. How to unarm my defenses. Let me be me. I've really missed you."

"You don't have to miss me anymore. I'm here, Tiff. For as long as you want me to be here."

She smiled at him. "I think that's going to be a very long time."

Braxton placed tender nip-kisses around the corners of her mouth.

"Might as well start now. What you got planned for the day?"

Tiffany threw her hand in the air. "After this crazy weekend, rest and relaxation for real."

"I hear ya," Braxton sighed. "This proposal really pushed me."

"Same here. What you got going on today?" Tiffany asked.

"Gotta do some work around the house. Church later on tonight."

"Church sounds good."

"My dad's doing a series on faith all week."

"A revival?"

"I wouldn't say that. It's more like a cram course. He does them every now and then. He records them, puts them on the church website so when he's preaching a sermon on Sunday, he can refer people to the classes if they don't have the basics under their belt already."

"That's neat. I'll have to check them out," Tiffany

said.

Braxton nearly bragged, "I've heard my father preach faith all my life, but never like this. Talking about the people in the Bible with unexpected faith: the woman with the issue of blood, the Centurion, the thief at the cross—people who weren't necessarily learned or skilled in the scriptures or even in right-standing with God but believed who Jesus is and put their faith in Him alone. It's amazing."

Tiffany said, "I hope you see yourself in those people, Braxton."

"Hmph." Braxton's body jerked. "That'll preach."

Tiffany poured a capful of bubble bath in the running water. *Why not two?* She followed the whim and poured another. She'd been waiting on this moment for days. Weeks. Probably months.

Time alone with her thoughts. No clients blowing up her phone. No drama from her family. Only the warm water, the mountain of bubbles, and thoughts of her morning with Braxton trickling through her mind.

As she slid into the tub, she mused, "This must be what it's like to be in love." She rested her head on the bath pillow. *Maybe, one day, Braxton and I can do this. Together.*

The thought made her stomach tingle and actually surprised her. *Am I turning into a hoochie?*

Trying to separate lust from what might be the beginnings of a life-long love seemed nearly impossible. How could she, when Braxton was so handsome? His voice so deep, his hands so strong.

Maybe if she concentrated on the words he said rather than the perfect lips they came from, that would help. She tried to focus on the words alone: *You don't have to miss me anymore. I'm here, Tiff. For as long as you want me to be here.*

Didn't work. Still too sexy.

How am I supposed to keep my mind off this man?

She got no answer in the tub or later on when she posed the question again in prayer. The attraction surrounded her even as she slept. This was not good. Or was it?

Maybe, like everything else that was playing out with Braxton, this was exactly how it was meant to be.

Chapter 21

The email came directly from Mr. McDonald Monday night. He wanted to see Braxton in his office first thing Tuesday morning. 8:15.

No sooner than he read the message, his phone was glowing with a local call. Though he hadn't saved her name in his phone, he recognized the number as Deja's. "Yel-lllo."

"Did you get the same email I got?" she blared.

"I'm…not sure."

"They've decided to go with another company," Deja mocked.

"No. I didn't get that email."

"Oh," she hesitated. "So I guess they picked you over me."

Braxton suggested, "Or Tiffany."

"Tiffany? Please. Don't make me laugh. It *must* be you."

"Perhaps."

"Well," she smacked, "if they did choose you, it would be in your best interest to partner up with Langley. Red Sea had a lot of personnel problems. Helping fire and hire the right people is going to require a working knowledge of current H-R laws."

"No, thank you, Deja. This is the end of the line for you and me."

"It doesn't have to be," she purred. "Now that the

professionalism is over, we could make it all pleasure. That is, if you're not too busy with Tiffany."

"I'm *very* busy with Tiffany, actually. Not that it's any of your business."

"Braxton, get real. Tiffany's a lesbian."

"What?"

"Yep. She worked at Langley for years. Never once have I seen her with a man. She never brought a man to any of our Christmas parties. Only her female *friends*. Really, I think she's just too tall for men. And too athletic-looking. Poor thing, probably didn't have much of a choice except to go that way. It's only a matter of time before she comes out of the closet."

Braxton stared at his phone incredulously. "Have you been smoking *crack* today?"

"I'm telling you what I know. She's not on our team."

"Bye, Felecia."

He eclipsed the call, blocked Deja's number, and threw her accusations right out the other side of his ear. *That girl is desperate.* He'd been around drama and seen enough clips from female reality shows to recognize when someone was trying to pump him with game.

Deja's foolishness aside, he had a better picture of what might happen tomorrow. He thought about calling Tiffany, but he stopped just shy of pressing the phone icon. What if Tiffany hadn't gotten a message? What if they had already informed her that he'd won? Or that *she'd* won?

He didn't want to be the one to have to break bad news or receive bad news from Tiffany. The best thing, he decided, was to show up and hear the verdict firsthand rather than speculate. Braxton rested that night knowing that whatever happened was in God's hands.

That assurance gave him and propelled him through a morning workout. He showered, dressed in a dark suit with a purple shirt, and rolled up to the Red Sea Academy singing and thanking God in advance for what He was doing.

Tiffany's car was in the Red Sea parking lot. *What's she doing here, too?*

Braxton stared at the vehicle for a second to make sure it was hers. Same gray interior. Same black mug sitting in the cup holder. *Yep, she's here.*

Inside the building, he searched Rhonda's face for a hint. *Does she know who got it?* "Morning, Rhonda."

"Morning, Braxton. Mr. McDonald said to send you right on in."

"Great."

Tiffany was nowhere in sight. *Did she get here at 8:00? Is he meeting with both of us together?*

Anxiety swelled in his stomach as he walked down the hallway. Only a week ago, he'd been reunited with Tiffany in this space. *It's all good*, he told himself.

Jeff McDonald was waiting in the smaller conference room, along with Tiffany, who was dressed in a magnificent animal print top. Her lips shined red.

"Morning, Braxton."

Braxton shook Jeff's hand. "Morning." He shook Tiffany's too, searching her face for a clue.

"Morning." Her face was locked with professionalism.

Braxton sat. Mr. McDonald closed the door.

"I'm so glad you were both able to come." He resumed his position at head. "You two made it very hard to choose. Your presentations were stellar, and the staff had very nice things to say about your mannerisms. Impressive. But as you know, we're only hiring one company to do the job."

Braxton glanced at Tiffany.

She kept focused on Mr. McDonald, but the vein pulsing heavily at her temple gave her away.

"The reason I decided to make the announcement with both of you present is because I wanted to make it clear that we might use either one of you at any time for future projects. Our school is expanding, we've got major milestones on the calendar. This won't be our last encounter, I'm sure of it."

Braxton and Tiffany nodded.

"Oh, and I have your checks for your service last week. Your notes alone were worth every penny."

He gave them their envelopes, followed by their thanks.

Mr. McDonald cleared his throat. "We've decided to go with Braxton-Gable-Stoneworth on this one."

"Congratulations," Tiffany quickly said, her hand ready for a congratulatory shake.

"Thank you," Braxton managed to say despite the fact that his heart broke for Tiffany in a way he hadn't anticipated.

She grabbed her computer case and purse. "I'll leave you two to get started."

"Thank you, Miss Warren," Mr. McDonald said, shaking her hand as well. "We'll be in touch when we need your services."

All that work for nothing!

Tiffany was having a hard time keeping her composure. She *wished* a pig would come running down the hallway today—she'd handle that pink thing!

Her heels clicked harder as she passed Rhonda's desk. "Have a good day."

"You, too," Tiffany chirped. She felt like the runner-up in a Miss America contest, standing there fake-crying next to the winner. Trying to be gracious while her dreams crumpled simultaneously. *This is bogus!*

She sat in her car for a second. Took some breaths. If she was going to cry, she certainly didn't want to do it on campus. Tiffany took off down the road, not really sure of where she might go from there. The only other project she had going was at a bit of a standstill. With the Thanksgiving holiday in just a few weeks, people were starting to take vacations here and there. It would only get worse in December—parties, fundraisers, more time off. All of that would mean less billable hours for her.

I'm going to go broke. Lose my apartment. Have to move back in with Mom. Get a job I don't like. Listen to my sisters say 'I told you so.'

The thoughts kept bombarding her. *My father would be so disappointed. This is terrible. My whole life is falling apart.*

She pulled up to the back side of a grocery store and threw her very own pity-party, complete with a nose as red as a clown's and mascara streamers flowing down her cheeks.

Tiffany's peripheral vision caught the light on the phone sitting in the passenger's seat.

Braxton was calling

"Go away!" she shouted at the device.

The party carried on in full swing until she invited the Lord. "God, I don't understand. I thought Red Sea was going to be my turning point. I mean, I did my best. Jeff McDonald even said so. Braxton doesn't even need money like I do—his dad is rich."

Her only party guest spoke in her heart: *You don't think I'm rich?*

She sniffed. "Yes. You are."

You don't think I have a good plan and a good future for you at the Red Sea Academy?

Tiffany's hands froze on the steering wheel, realizing that God was giving a personalized version of Jeremiah 29:11 inside her. She had to admit: Running into Braxton had been good. The proposal experience was beneficial. She could probably call Mr. McDonald and ask him about the weak points. He'd surely let her know. She did have a nice check to cash. And the kids...they had given her plenty of laughs and even hope for the future with their inquisitive, brilliant minds.

Plans and hope for the future.

This pity party was over.

Tiffany put her car in drive and backtracked to the Red Sea Academy.

Chapter 22

Braxton hadn't been able to get in touch with Tiffany since he saw her at Red Sea. She wasn't returning calls or even texts, though his phone showed they had been successfully delivered. He convinced himself that Tiffany just needed some time to process the loss. Yet, her distance disturbed him. How would she act now that he'd won? What if she decided to stop seeing him? Was the contract worth losing her again? Would he want to be with a woman who took business so personally?

He listened as the praise team worshipped the Lord in song, led by West. The sweet-sounding soprano, Ijoni, was a shapely sister with natural ringlets that flowed past her shoulders. She was pretty. Loved the church, came from a great family. Braxton had even called her once, but she was...*how had he said it?*...too into him. She laughed before he delivered his punch lines, said "yes" before he'd finished asking his questions.

She might as well have been a Lambda Nu Queen.

But Tiffany. She listened, she heard, she thought, she answered. She laughed, too, but not until something was actually funny. And Braxton was intrigued by her what-you-see-is-what-you-get appearance. Seeing her dressed up and made up was a special treat, but there was no fear of what he might discover when she took off her hair, makeup and fake body parts.

Nobody was better than Tiffany. Period.

The praise team concluded its segment and Braxton's father took the podium.

"Turn your Bibles to the book of Hebrews, chapter eleven. We're going to take a walk around the hall of faith tonight."

Braxton settled into the scriptures and took notes as his father called the roll of the faithful, from Abel all the way to Samuel and the prophets.

This God who had forgiven King David of horrible offenses had also forgiven him. Braxton already knew that he was forgiven. He'd convinced himself that the problem was misleading others. He was familiar enough with his shortcomings and knew that he would never be a perfect leader. The temptation to turn to alcohol came back here and again. What if he went to the ten-year-reunion and got drunk again? Got another DUI and went to jail? Then he'd have to go to prison. What would happen to his witness? His father's ministry? Ultimately, would people turn away from God, be eternally lost because of him?

"In this list of faith giants," his father honed in on the night's message, "we find a name that some would find questionable. In verse thirty-two. Samson. By all accounts, he was amazingly strong but quick to anger. And his one weakness was a woman."

The congregation murmured with a few chortles.

Deacon Williams shouted out, "Preach, sir!" to which the church body laughed at the single brother.

"Deacon, we'll talk later," Pastor Stoneworth said.

They all laughed again.

As Reth Braxton expounded on the word, taking them back to the book of Judges, Braxton found himself in Samson. An imperfect man with a specific weakness. And even though Samson actually ended up having to kill himself, somehow God deemed Samson's heart faithful, worthy to be listed amongst...well, when Braxton flipped back to the list, he couldn't find a perfect one among the names. Because Braxton knew the scriptures, he knew Abraham, Moses, Sarah, Rahab—none of them was perfect.

And yet, as his father spoke, the Word illuminated the Truth for Braxton in a way that he had never understood it before. God wasn't requiring him to be perfect, only willing and humble enough to lean on Him. Even when he messed up along the journey, God would still count him faithful as he repented and made corrections along the way. This is life.

He'd heard it once from Tiffany. Then from his father. Now in the Word.

How many more times does God have to say this?

When his father made the altar call, Braxton walked toward the center aisle with his hands raised in surrender. He was the third person in line.

Braxton felt a hand on his back and looked to his

right. His mother had come to agree with his request. Braxton hugged her slightly. She stayed at his side as he approached his father.

"How can I pray for you, son?"

"I want God to give me the wisdom, strength, and boldness to do His will," Braxton stated.

His father smiled. "He said in His word that He gives wisdom without reproach and liberally to all who ask. The righteous are as bold as lions. And He gives strength to those that wait on him," Braxton's dad quoted.

As his father spoke, the actual scripture references came to Braxton's mind: James 1:5, Proverbs 28:1, Isaiah 40:31. This gift of understanding and remembering scriptures had to be shared with other believers—he'd never been more sure of it.

Both Braxton's parents laid hands on him and prayed for exactly what Braxton knew was promised in the Word.

In faith, he received it.

That settled it.

Tiffany had seen where Braxton was sitting before he joined the prayer line. While the preacher and a woman whose skin color and bone structure gave her away as Braxton's mom prayed for him, Tiffany inched up a few rows closer to the front. Truthfully, she wanted to run up there and pray for him, too, but that might look a little weird.

Instead, she'd bowed her head and asked the Lord to honor Braxton's request, whatever it was.

God had most definitely honored hers.

Braxton returned to his seat in deep thought, his head still bowed.

With the congregation still in praise and worship and the building rather sparse, Tiffany was able to make it all the way to the pew behind him. A seasoned lady wearing an oversized sweater welcomed Tiffany with a hug.

"You a visitor?"

"Yes, ma'am."

"Glad to have you."

"Thank you."

Now sure that she wouldn't miss Braxton after the benediction, Tiffany lifted her hands and joined in corporate worship with the house. Her soul felt like it was filling up with a tall glass of lemonade on a hot, dusty day.

The praise team started a quick number, which put the congregation in a joyous mood for dismissal. Tiffany clapped along to an upbeat tempo, tickled to be standing behind Braxton without him knowing it.

A minister spoke into the microphone while they were still standing. "Since we're all up, we might as well go ahead and give the benediction so we can go in peace."

"Amen!"

The music faded.

"Why don't you go ahead and grab the hand of

the person standing next to you."

The older lady started to reach for Braxton's hand, but Tiffany wasn't having it. She whipped that left hand up and caught Braxton before he could be touched by anyone else.

His eyes traveled up her hand to her face.

She smiled. "Hi."

Braxton's eyes nearly twinkled with excitement. He pulled her around to his row.

"Mmmm hmmm," Tiffany's former pew-mate hummed. "Go on, chile."

Tiffany stood next to Braxton, whose teeth seemed to almost pop out of his head. He was going overboard with the happiness.

"Now may the Holy Spirit rest, rule and abide in each of us until we meet again. Let all the church sing..."

"Aaaaa-men."

Tiffany had barely finished her "*men*" when Braxton started in on her. "Tiff, I've been calling you all day. What happened? Where have you been?"

She squeezed his hand. "I left. I was hurt. But then I talked to God about it. Thought about how happy I was to be around kids. How hopeful. How ecstatic. So I went back and asked Mr. McDonald if there was any way I could teach there."

"Seriously?"

"Yeah." Tiffany explained, "He said there's a teacher going out on maternity leave next semester. I could come on as her replacement in January. I need to take some classes and get my certification in the next year or so, but he said that me becoming a part of the Red Sea faculty would be an answer to his prayer, too."

"Wow. This is amazing. For both of us," Braxton buzzed. "God has opened both our eyes to some awesome things today."

"I know, right?"

"Man, I wish we weren't in this church so I could kiss you."

"Braaaaax-ton," Tiffany cooed. Her belly turned to mush.

His father and mother interrupted the conversation. "Son, you going to introduce us to your acquaintance?"

"She sure is lovely," his mother remarked.

"Thank you," Tiffany accepted the compliment.

Now that she was up close and personal with Braxton's parents, Tiffany could see that his mother was basically the short version of Braxton with lighter skin, and obviously the source of his dark eyelashes. She also appeared to be much younger than his father, although it was always hard to tell with an African-American woman.

"Tiffany, these are my parents, Reth and Carolyn Stoneworth. Mom and Dad, this is Tiffany Warren. My lady."

His mother smiled in a teasing manner and looked up at her husband.

His father squinted. "Is she the one who talked

some sense into you about the D-N-A?"

Braxton tilted his head. "Yeah, Dad, she's the one, but I don't think this is the place or the time for that conversation."

"It's always time for the Truth. Good to meet you young lady."

"Same here." Tiffany greeted Braxton's parents with a handshake. "I enjoyed the sermon."

"Glad it blessed you. Come again any time."

"Sure will."

Quickly, Braxton whisked Tiffany outside.

"Where are we going?"

"You'll see." He unlocked his truck, practically threw her inside.

"Braxton, what are we doing?"

He hopped into his seat, drove out of the parking lot, then abruptly stopped at the shopping center next door.

"Ummm…why are we here?"

"Because I want to kiss you."

Tiffany surmised, "But not on church grounds."

"Right.

"I'll bet you said that to all the girls you kissed on the side of the church," Tiffany teased.

"True dat," he admitted with a silly grin on his face.

Tiffany busted out laughing.

"I've done a lot of stuff wrong, but I've never disrespected the house of God. I don't want to kiss you in that building until…" he raised an eyebrow.

"I know," Tiffany gave him some leeway. It was way too soon to be talking the M-word. Besides, she didn't want him to mention that word to her unless he had a ring in his back pocket.

Braxton tapped the tip of her nose. Pecked her lips. "I'm crazy about you. When you didn't call me back today, I was lost. Like I'd missed the winning shot in double overtime with no time left on the clock."

Tiffany traced his cheek with her thumb. "You don't have to miss me anymore, Braxton. I'm here. In a way, I've always been waiting for you, I think. It's like maybe I was stuck on you. I'm not going to run away from you again. If I leave again, it'll—"

Braxton snuffed her words with a kiss. "Don't. 'Cause I'm stuck on you, too."

Tiffany squirmed. "So what do we do now? I've never been in a *real* real relationship with anyone."

"Come to think of it, I've never been in a truly *godly* relationship with anyone long-term. This is new for me, too. To be honest, I don't wanna mess this up."

"Me, either. But I don't think we can move forward if we're fearful. We just have to let God lead us," Tiffany suggested.

Braxton raised his hand like a student in a classroom.

"Yes."

"Step number one is, you're going to have to stop wearing that perfume. It's breaking me down. Who gave it to you—Deja?"

Tiffany punched his arm, "No you didn't!"

He covered his face. "I bet it's called Delilah, ain't it?"

"Whatever! Take me back on the church grounds to my car, please."

Braxton's deep laugh filled the car as he put the car in Drive.

Tiffany breathed in their joy.

You are so good, God. So good.

Epilogue

Tiffany and Braxton sat side-by-side at the head table, nearly drunk with their own love and joy as they looked out on a sea of faces who were celebrating his parents' thirtieth anniversary. In just a few months, many of these same people would gather again for Tiffany and Braxton's wedding.

Braxton leaned toward her ear. "You ready for this?"

"Can't happen soon enough for me," Tiffany said. Since she had begun teaching and gotten engaged in the same month, things had been a whirlwind—a fun whirlwind, nothing like the overwhelming feelings she'd battled when she was trying to start her own business.

Granted, she was still a workaholic, but now she could see the long-term effects of her work: hope and a future for herself as well as her students.

The New Year's Day engagement came as a surprise with Braxton halting his family's dinner for an announcement. Tiffany had thought maybe he was going to tell his family the news that he had filed the paperwork to start his non-profit ministry and publishing company aimed at sharing the gospel with young men—an often neglected sector of the population.

But instead, he had nearly caused Tiffany to

choke on her black-eyed peas when he dropped down on one knee and whipped out a ring. His family roared and whistled like they were at a football game.

"Tiffany Warren, will you do me the honor of becoming my wife."

She could hardly see the ring for the tears in her eyes. "Yes!"

They'd wanted a small wedding, but with Pastor Stoneworth's prominence came a long list of people to invite. "We've been giving gifts and money to these people's kids for graduations, weddings, and baby showers all these years. Now it's their turn to bless our family," Tiffany's future mother-in-law had insisted. Tiffany didn't complain since her in-laws deemed it only fair to contribute to the cost of the wedding since they were running up the guest count with all of their professional and pastoral acquaintances.

Now, as she sat listening to her soon-to-be father-in-law, Tiffany was so proud to be a part of Braxton's life. Their relationship had already endured its first major test. When the D-N-A results arrived in the mail, Braxton had called Tiffany to come meet him. "I missed the delivery. I have to pick up the envelope at the UPS center before nine. Can you meet me there?"

"No problem."

Tiffany had prayed through the whole drive. To be honest, she kind of hoped Brianna wasn't his. Then she wouldn't have to do the step-mother thing.

But she repented of her selfishness and prayed instead for Braxton, whose heart must have felt torn at the moment. "God, give him strength to get through this."

After Braxton signed in with his name and address, they waited for his name to be called along with a dozen other people in the cold, steel building.

"Stoneworth!" the dark-haired man called with a Spanish accent.

"Right here." Braxton signed for the oversized envelope. "Thank you."

He and Tiffany walked to his truck in silence. Got inside.

"I can't open it," he said.

Tiffany took the package from his trembling hands. She tore through the seal. "No matter what this paper says, Braxton, the results are not a surprise to God."

He rocked his chin up and down in agreement. He grabbed her forearm and squeezed. "Let's do this."

Tiffany slid the papers from the envelope, searched the first few lines to make sense of the results, and saw the answer. "Braxton, Brianna is not your daughter."

He covered his eyes. "Mmmph." His jaw clenched.

"I'm so sorry, honey."

To her surprise, Tiffany's own emotions bubbled to the surface, wetting her face.

"Mmmph," Braxton repeated. He finally removed his hands and looked at Tiffany again. "Then who *is* her father? Who's going to send her a Christmas gift next year? Tell her to stay away from bootleg jokers? Walk her down the aisle?"

"I don't know. Let's just pray about it. If Alicia doesn't know who her father is…there's no reason you can't still *care* about Brianna. I mean, once someone's in your heart, they're in there, you know?"

"Yeah. I guess we both know that. Look at *us*."

Thankfully, Alicia had been able to locate and test Brianna's real father the following month. He was actually one of Braxton's frat brothers—a guy named Lester who had been Braxton's "big brother." Braxton and Lester had been in touch. Though they hadn't worked out any particulars, it seemed as though Lester wanted to be in his daughter's life, and he looked forward to Braxton's sideline participation as well, at least until Brianna was old enough to comprehend what was happening.

Braxton's parents were now grandchild-less again, something that his father had mentioned more than once.

He'd hinted, even at this thirty-fifth anniversary party, that he was looking forward to the day he could take his grandson fishing, eyeing Braxton and his brothers, though he steered clear of looking at Rainey and her guest, Elvin.

No sooner Reth Stoneworth said, "I hope to have my grands here when we celebrate the fortieth," a clap of thunder caused the lights to flicker momentarily.

"See. Even God agrees with me," he joked.

Tiffany and Braxton smiled at one another. They'd already decided to start on their family as soon as possible.

When the live gospel band fired up the music again, Reth practically pulled his wife, kicking and screaming, onto the dance floor for their traditional hokey-pokey dance.

Tiffany was just about to ask Braxton why on earth his parents were doing that crazy dance when he pulled her onto the floor as well. Soon, they were flanked with a host of other friends and family members who suspended all sense while putting their heads in and their heads out and turning themselves about.

Braxton made up silly moves with each turn, always the life of the party. With the way the rain was pouring down outside, it was possible they might all be stuck inside for hours dancing, which was just fine with Tiffany. She was grateful to have Braxton in her life, bringing his own brand of joy, humor, and wisdom in the most unexpected moments. Their relationship had been a long time coming, but she planned to enjoy every second they had together from now until forever.

If you enjoyed Stuck On You,
Be sure to follow my blog
(MichelleStimpson.com) to be notified of new
releases!

All This Love
Book #2 in the Stoneworth Series

Scheduled for release - Spring 2016!

*Will Knox Stoneworth be able to move past his
humiliating heartbreak
and fall in love again?*

Discussion Questions

1. The Stoneworth family has a rich history that is passed down from one generation to the next. Braxton felt a strong need to uphold his family name and, more importantly, his faith. What motivates you?

2. Tiffany was afraid of animals. What are you afraid of? Have you ever let that fear stand in the way of something you wanted?

3. Braxton doesn't think he'll be able to handle it if Tiffany wins the contract over him. What's your take on his feelings? Do you think most men struggle with their own insecurities with regard to women who are professionally successful?

4. Tiffany has gotten into the habit of relying on energy drinks to make it through her busy days. Do you think this is a problem? In the past, how have you made it through busy seasons in your life?

5. Tiffany thinks she might be losing respect for Braxton if he's a deadbeat dad. Is a man's relationship with his kids an indication of whether or not he's good relationship material?

6. In the past, Tiffany has steered clear of a man with any kind of record. Is that a good policy?

Is there any type of crime that you're willing to overlook before dating someone? What if a person has done their time and is free—would you be willing to consider a romantic relationship with an ex-con? Why or why not?

7. Tiffany says she's no stranger to "staging around temptation." Is it possible for single Christians to set up their relationships so that they avoid compromising situations?

8. In her mind, Tiffany usually thinks of the Red Sea's CEO as "Mr. McDonald", but Braxton often thinks of him as "Jeff McDonald." Do you think that women have a hard time subconsciously overcoming traditional roles in the workplace, particularly in male-dominated fields?

9. Tiffany's older sister got upset when Tiffany kissed Braxton in front of her teenage niece. Did you see this as a problem? Why or why not? What did you think of Tiffany's talk with Madison?

10. Braxton went overboard regarding his affiliation with a fraternity. Do you know people who go overboard about sports teams? Celebrities? Even church affiliation? What makes us so excited about being a part of something bigger than ourselves? Is this simply a natural inclination or is it our soul's cry to connect with an Almighty God?

11. Do you ever feel that your siblings or older

family members are overstepping their boundaries? How do you handle them in love?

12. After the argument with Braxton, Tiffany repented for gossiping in order to entertain. Is there a difference between "making fun of people" and "gossip"? If so, where do you draw the line? Where does the Bible draw the line?

13. At Sunday lunch, Cassie tells Tiffany that she needs to start accepting help. Are you good at receiving help?

14. Braxton says he wants a woman who can cook, and he went so far as to take Tiffany to a cooking class. What are your absolutes for a mate? How would you have felt if the person you were falling in love with took you to a class to learn how to do something he/she wants you to do?

15. Braxton recognized right away that Deja was only trying to undermine his relationship when Deja insisted that Tiffany was gay. Do you immediately recognize when you are being manipulated by others? How do you respond—tit for tat, or simply end the conversation?

16. When Rainey called and told her older brothers that she was bringing home a guest, they immediately became protective. Did you find their reaction endearing or annoying?

17. Tiffany was a master at keeping her

professional composure. Do you have a game-face for work? For other places? When does the "face" become a harmful mask?

18. Braxton feared joining his father's ministry because he was afraid that he would ultimately cause others to fall away from the Lord. What does this tell you about Braxton's character? If you're hesitant to assume your calling, what holds you back? Are there scriptures that speak to your fears? What will happen if you *don't* heed your calling?

More Books by Michelle Stimpson

Christian Fiction

A Forgotten Love (Novella) Book One in the "A Few Good Men" Series

The Start of a Good Thing (Novella) Book Two in the "A Few Good Men" Series

A Shoulda Woulda Christmas (Novella)

Boaz Brown (Book 1 in the Boaz Brown Series)

No Weapon Formed (Book 2 in the Boaz Brown Series)

Divas of Damascus Road

Falling into Grace

I Met Him in the Ladies' Room (Novella)

I Met Him in the Ladies' Room Again (Novella)

Last Temptation

Mama B: A Time to Speak (Book 1)

Mama B: A Time to Dance (Book 2)

Mama B: A Time to Love (Book 3)

Mama B: A Time to Mend (Book 4)

Mama B: A Time for War (Book 5)

Mama B: A Time to Plant (Book 6)

Someone to Watch Over Me

Stepping Down

The Good Stuff

The Blended Blessings Series (co-authored with CaSandra McLaughlin)

Trouble In My Way (Young Adult)

What About Momma's House? Series (Novellas with April Barker)

Non-Fiction

Did I Marry the Wrong Guy? And other silent ponderings of a fairly normal Christian wife

Uncommon Sense: 30 Truths to Radically Renew Your Mind in Christ

The 21-Day Publishing Plan

If you like Michelle Stimpson's books, you'll want to meet her literary friends!

BlackChristianReads.com

About the Author

Michelle Stimpson's numerous works include the highly acclaimed *Boaz Brown*, *Divas of Damascus Road* (National Bestseller), the award-winning Mama B series, and *Falling Into Grace*, which has been optioned for a movie of the week. She has published several short stories for high school students through her educational publishing company at WeGottaRead.com.

Michelle serves in women's ministry at her home church, Oak Cliff Bible Fellowship. She regularly speaks at special events and writing workshops sponsored churches, schools, book clubs, and educational organizations.

The Stimpsons are proud parents of two young adults—one in the military, one in college—and a weird Cocker Spaniel named MiMi.

Visit Michelle online:
www.MichelleStimpson.com
www.Facebook.com/michelle.stimpson2

9.99

1/17

LONGWOOD PUBLIC LIBRARY
800 Middle Country Road
Middle Island, NY 11953
(631) 924-6400
longwoodlibrary.org

LIBRARY HOURS

Monday-Friday	9:30 a.m. - 9:00 p.m.
Saturday	9:30 a.m. - 5:00 p.m.
Sunday (Sept-June)	1:00 p.m. - 5:00 p.m.

65476454R00148

Made in the USA
Charleston, SC
20 December 2016